displacement

displacement

THALIA CHALTAS

An Imprint of Penguin Group (USA) Inc.

VIKING
Published by Penguin Group
Penguin Group (USA) Inc., 345 Hudson Street, New York, New York 10014, U.S.A.
Penguin Group (Canada), 90 Eglinton Avenue East, Suite 700, Toronto, Ontario,
Canada M4P 2Y3 (a division of Pearson Penguin Canada Inc.)
Penguin Books Ltd, 80 Strand, London WC2R 0RL, England
Penguin Ireland, 25 St Stephen's Green, Dublin 2, Ireland (a division of Penguin Books Ltd)
Penguin Group (Australia), 250 Camberwell Road, Camberwell, Victoria 3124,
Australia (a division of Pearson Australia Group Pty Ltd)
Penguin Books India Pvt Ltd, 11 Community Centre, Panchsheel Park,
New Delhi – 110 017, India
Penguin Group (NZ), 67 Apollo Drive, Rosedale, North Shore 0632, New Zealand
(a division of Pearson New Zealand Ltd.)
Penguin Books (South Africa) (Pty) Ltd, 24 Sturdee Avenue, Rosebank,
Johannesburg 2196, South Africa

Penguin Books Ltd, Registered Offices: 80 Strand, London WC2R 0RL, England

First published in 2011 by Viking, a member of Penguin Group (USA) Inc.

1 3 5 7 9 10 8 6 4 2

LIBRARY OF CONGRESS CATALOGING-IN-PUBLICATION DATA

Chaltas, Thalia.
Displacement / by Thalia Chaltas.
p. cm.
Summary: After tragedy strikes her family, Vera runs away to a small desert town
where she tries unsuccessfully to forget her grief and sorrow.
ISBN 978-0-670-01199-5 (hardcover)
[1. Novels in verse. 2. Grief—Fiction. 3. Death—Fiction. 4. Sisters—Fiction.
5. Deserts—Fiction. 6. Pottery—Fiction.] I. Title.
PZ7.5.C48Di 2011 [Fic]—dc22 2010044305

Printed in U.S.A. Set in Berkeley Oldstyle Book design by Nancy Brennan

To Styliani Munroe,

who has come through many displacements

and keeps finding her place again

displacement

Miracle Whip on white,
American cheese,
a crunchy tomato slab.
The desert's veggie sandwich.

I'm wolfing it down.
Been a long-ass day
and it's only
lunchtime.

SaraJane plants her
massive breasts on top of her forearm
flat on the counter,
batwinging her fake eyelashes at me.

"Good, ain't it, hon?
Made it myself.
Where you headed?"

The short version is a wave of my hand and
"Up toward Lone Pine."

The eyelashes flash open,
trapping penciled-on eyebrows
against her skin.

"There's no bus that direction from here, hon.
Lemme check with Virgil."
And she's swishing off and yelling to
some trucker and his wife
I need a ride.

Which, hell, I do.
I guess.

I only thought out
getting to the desert.

Here I am.

On a whim
I buy two postcards
of SaraJane's Eats
before we all climb in.

Truck cabs are huge!
The AC cranked,
Virgil, Belle, and I
sing country western songs one after another—
what luck to get this ride.

"No offense, doll,
but I'm surprised you know these songs!" Virgil says.

I turn to the window.
The words come out without thinking.
"My sister loved them."

They don't ask.

After a few hours of driving,

Virg and Belle need to take
a quick detour before Lone Pine
to pick up somethingorother for a friend.
Gearing down, we turn up a lonely length of
road
that somehow looks
promising to me.

And when we crest a small mountain
the pile of sand by a tumbling wooden structure
catches my interest.

"Is that a mine?" I ask.

"Two Shanks Mine. Gold and silver.
That's what started the town of Garrett."

"Garrett? Can you drop me there?"
An old gold mining town . . .

I smell geology.

The semi slows and sits at grumbling idle.
"Here y'are!
Garrett's over that rise.
Not allowed to take rigs on that road.
You'll have to walk from here."

I grab my pack.

"Sure you'll be okay?
Not much to Garrett,"
Belle says
as I clack the door open and
    jump down into surprising cool.

"She'll be fine," I hear Virgil mutter.

"This is great!
Thank you so much!"

"Best of luck, doll!"

And I wave through the roar and gravel

as they haul off.

A moment of silence
and my phone rings.
I turn it off without looking.

I tuck a wild curl behind my ear.

Shoulder straps on,
I march onto the side road,
following the sign.

➔ GARRETT—2 MILES

Cool air up at elevation.

Still, I'm hot walking
in jeans.

Just as I get a good rhythm in my head
I round a bend
and the valley below
splays before me
in afternoon heat-shimmers
like corrugated cardboard,
dots of brown
blocky houses
scattered
in the dirt.

I can just make out a sign—
    the something "Inn"—
over a squat building
along the main road.
At least there's a place
to stay tonight.

A heated gust staggers me
and I grin at the unsheltered town of Garrett
flat against the slope
but hidden in all directions.

Here nobody knows me.

She's laughing at me.
"What kinda job you think
we got in thith plathe?"
Rocking her fat ass back in her chair
 she howls like the oven-hot wind outside,
the gap of a broken black incisor
 showering spit.

I rub my bare arm.
Wind slings gravel
 under the rattling Mercantile door.
"I can cook?" I say too softly.

She's still gurgling mirth,
 scalp shining through
 spider silk hair
"Job . . ." she repeats,
wiping her eyes.

I can crochet, too, lady,
 but it's 115 degrees out and I can't face
 the saliva rain again.

Horizontal window smears
match flying debris
sandblasting a painted block wall:

DISTRIBUTOR FOR ATLAS POWDER CO.
EVERYTHING FOR BLASTING

"I know about rocks and stuff."
Yeah. Brilliantly said
for someone accepted for geology at Stanford.

Tilly tips forward
eyes suddenly still and clear.
"Well, now. That'th thomething. But a mining
town,
we know more'n a young girl already."

Huh.
I tighten my bandanna over hair
already leaden with sand.

“Well, this ‘young girl’ needs a job.
Can you help me or not?”

Tilly taps a grimy nail
on the rocker’s arm,
watching a pebble dance merrily
across the wooden floor.

“I’ll check with thomeone.
Mebbe tomorrow.”

She launches forward
heaving to her feet.

“Now.
You’re hungry.
The chili’th real good,”
and she ushers me to the
Mercantile counter
where I have a decidedly

submediocre
evening meal of heated Hormel chili
with dried onions
on top.

When I ask about staying at the Miner's Inn,
Tilly waves her hand at me.

"He'll want to charge you."

"Well it can't be that expensive this far out—"

Raising her arm so the underflap dangles
dangerously
close to my chin,
Tilly waves vaguely to the west.

"Jutht find one for thale.
Plenty of 'em."

What?

"I don't want to buy a house, Tilly.
I just need a room."

She roars like a chubby lioness.

"They all left. 'Houthe for Thale' meanth
they're gone. Not really thelling it."

She takes my shoulders
steering me out the Mercantile's door.

"Plenty of choitheth. No one will bother you."

I am out in the wind,
rocks biting my ankles.

Just move into someone's house?

"They all left,"
    I hear her say behind me.

It takes me an hour to get up the guts.

I look at all the "For Sale" houses
trying to keep to ones without
actual neighbors because—
well, because somehow
this is now embarrassing?

And when I find the little chocolate wood-sided
cabin
peering out from behind
two bigger places,
I look around quickly
and make myself try the dented brass knob.

A comfortable click,
and the door swings
with a short shuddering
but no ominous creak like I expected.

From the front door,
three rooms.

Living room.
Bedroom.
Kitchenette sort of alcove off the living room.

I close myself in.

Not much furniture left.
Low coffee table with a small blue vase.
Woodstove that I wouldn't begin to know how
to use.
Vinyl chair at the fake marble Formica counter.
Two plates, one mug, fry pan, pot, three forks.
Bed with an old cotton mattress.
I lean in to sniff suspiciously
and the mattress seems okay.

The only other thing is a dresser,
the kind with a mirror attached on top.

In the bottom drawer is a wool blanket.
In the top drawer is a sheet,

which I take out and also sniff.

A whiff of cedar.

I whack the mattress gently
and shake out the sheet,
wafting it lightly over the bed
before tucking.

The last sheet corner has an intricately
embroidered *A*

and I sink to a kneel

at the foot of the bed

and cry for the first time.

I am curled on the bed
eyes swollen half shut
having sobbed myself out on the floor.

My mind feels numb
and I am trying not to recapture what I was
  thinking
as I cried.

I know Amy died, right?
This is not news. It's been almost a month.

    Crying doesn't help anything.

Gawd, I hated it when the Moth said that to us.
I hate that I even think it in her voice,
    silky sweet and gentle
    but the clear message to shut up.
Crying is not polite in the Moth's social world.

I propel myself off the bed
and into the teensy bathroom.

Turn the cold faucet with a squeal.

Let the water run

to clear the pipes.

Splash my face.

Thankful for a missing mirror over the sink.

"Milo Brandt."
Tilly hands me the slip of paper.
"He'th a theramithitht."
The spray from her gap sparkles forth
in the leaning morning light.

"A what?" I take a step back.

"Pottery!" she shrieks.
"He'th an artitht!
Bowlth, jugth, plateth,
thellth it all on the Internet."

Ceramicist,
that's what she is saying.
Is that a real word?

"A potter?"

"Maybe he needth help
running the pug mill."

I get a quick visual of
some kind of kennel
churning out pug puppies,
and raise my eyebrows.

"Like a mixther for clay," Tilly states.

Gawd.
Sounds lovely.

Trudging uphill toward Milo's,
watching dust poof
in soft explosions
around each step of my hiking boots.

How long do boots last in this climate?

And what do I know about pottery?

I was hoping
for a real job.

Something outside,
with rocks
and research.

Something where I can
use my brain.

“Nothing to burn, see?”
Milo flings a skinny arm
at the dryscape around us.
“Perfect place for
a twenty-two-hundred-degree kiln.”

He’s a Tweedledee-shaped man:
bulging pudgy body
and spidery limbs,
a soft voice
and raucous laugh.

He has all his teeth.

Came here from Needles
six years ago.

“Tilly mentioned a pug mill?”

He takes me to the shed
where a bulging pudgy-bodied machine
churns scrap clay

into usable material
with a ratcheting cackle.

I take a step backward.
"Maybe I could drive your orders
into Barville
to the post office?
You could keep working."

Milo scratches his scalp,
which shines gently in the damp of the shed.
"Could be.
Wouldn't be maybe only once per week."

It's a start.

I've named it the Hovel.

The cabin's très small,
a bit dingy
and dog-eared,
but it's mine
for now
and Hovel sounds just a bit
like
Home.

Bored, I pick up the bedraggled broom
and start sweeping the Mercantile.

"Can't pay you for that," Tilly mutters.

She says that every time.
Since I don't do that much for Milo yet
I need to keep myself occupied,
and I love sweeping.

A dually pulls up out front
scattering gravel.
Out piles a cadre of four guys
a bit older than me.
And then a fifth
slides out of the driver's seat,
lean and feral,
smoothly oiled.
Hand running over his long hair,
he turns casually
to look in the window,

locking eyes with me.
Raven eyes.
I'm caught.

"Oh," I say softly
and Tilly is at my back,
looking out.

"Hmp," she says,
treading heavily toward the back of the Merc.

As they come in the door,
the guys scatter,
each to a different area of the store.

Now I am on my guard.

Did they come to steal something?

Tilly sits solidly in the back,
not greeting them.

He comes in last,
smiling congenially,
    like sand sifting off the dune ridge,
and I find myself taking a step toward him
involuntarily.

"Can I help you?" I hear myself say
in the high social voice
of my mother.

His name is Lon,
and after he introduces me to everyone
the five guys are
lined up on the cracked round stools
at the counter
eating canned chili
like it's delicious homemade.

"So we've set up shop on my uncle's little spot
uphill from here,
Secondary Packaging," Lon is saying.
"Going pretty well."
He eyes me,
head tilted
Corvus-like.
"You should come see
how we work," he says warmly.

My mouth opens
but Tilly's firm voice rasps
"She'th *got* a job."

And on unspoken cue or something
they are sliding dollars under plates,
swooping out the door
as if Lon had gathered them
under a sleek dark wing.

I tramp to the Hovel
angrily kicking stones.

I acted like such a
smitten kitten
practically speechless,
letting Tilly answer for me.

Edging around the cactus
next to the steps
I tromp inside
and plunk on the living room floor
facing the coffee table.

I liked the plane of Lon's cheek,
chiseled by Native Americans,
relaxing for a wide laughing mouth.

I wonder which place is his uncle's.

Following thin animal trails
around a brump of brush,
a sudden broad dip in the mountainside
reveals
a mess of pickup trucks—

four, five, six of them
and an old gold Duster.

A cluster of four
mining company shacks
and a dented Airstream.

I feel jumpy,
but resolutely kick down the path
to call on the neighbors.

As my path melds
with dirt road,
someone opens the trailer's screen door,

raising a hand to see
through ripples of heat.

The hand raises in greeting
opening a brilliant smile
in lowering sun.

Lon.

My hands are folded
on the tiny Formica table.
I feel prim and pleasant
and all too Moth-ish,
but Lon is

breathtaking

and I am unmistakably nervous
in a way that's thrilling
and stupid.

"This Airstream is our office,"
he's saying.
"Accounting, paperwork,
boring stuff—that's my job."
The grin electrifies the surroundings.
A bit like an eel.

"And what do the other guys do?"
My voice comes to me

as if through a panel of glass,
swaddled and high.

"Everything else.
They're the worker bees.
Packaging, delivery—always on the go."

"Drones," I correct him without thinking.
Worker bees are female.

But he laughs, thinking
I'm making a joke.
Then he becomes serious,
leaning elbows on the table,
brown irises intense.
"What's your thing?
What's your passion?" he asks,
molten with sincerity.
And foolishly,
I start talking.

I don't think Lon
will care about my grades
and getting into Stanford.
But I'm proud of what I know
And can't help going on about
volcanic plugs
magma viscosity
and
rhyolitic lava,
sliding a little into my fave area,
Long Valley Caldera.

Lon is right with me
nodding seriously
getting more and more still
and I'm damn sure I'm impressing him.

One of the guys bursts in,
really frickin' irritating
in the middle of my demo
of geo prowess.

Lon shifts to greet him.
"Hey, Andrew,
you remember Vera?"
As I turn to shake hands
with the darkly native Andrew,
I flicker eyes to Lon
whose own eyes are
on me,
pensive.

And then
that smile flashes on,
Vegas neon, baby,
so genuine it hurts.

Guys on the coast are so easy to read.
I can tell if they like me
or not
pretty
quick.

But Lon seems complicated and cloistered,
his beautiful face
changing expression
every three seconds.

So I am a little shocked
when he says
in a bright tone
"So how about working for Secondary
  Packaging?"
with a big smile.

"What?" I say.

"Well, from what I've heard
you aren't doing much for Milo,

and I need to have someone
good with numbers
take over some paperwork
a few days a week
so I can attend other things."

The place doesn't look so rockin' busy
that he would need help,
but he's still wearing
that inviting grin,
and as he leans toward me,
my eyes are drawn to the pulse
above his collarbone
and
I find myself nodding.

Lon eases back,
his smile more relaxed,
nodding also.

"I treat my team well.
Good pay," he says,

his fingers stroking the skin of his forearm.

"How much?" I say crisply,
moving to the bench seat's edge.

Lon lets loose a great joyous laugh.
"Atta girl!" he crows,
clasping my shoulder
with his hand.
"I need a businesswoman like you."

As I pass him on the trail,
Dempsey glares and grumbles
through the scrubble beard
sprawled on his chin.

    I met him at the Mercantile yesterday.

    I said, "Good to meet you."
    Dempsey grunted.

I turn to watch him
stump in his boots uptrail.
He looks like a worn-out
surfer dude
    longish dirty-blond hair
    ruddy sunny skin
maybe the Moth's age.

Dempsey doesn't seem to like me.

That's okay.

I don't like his body odor or his
shock-orange T-shirt.

Super-happy-citrusy-safe-like-the-Coast-Guard
orange.

Shopping list:

ONIONS	CAN OF BEANS	CRUNCHY O'S CEREAL
POTATOES	FROZEN CHICKEN	EGG NOODLES

I miss my almond milk.
No one's even heard of it here.
Cereal with H_2O just plain sucks,
but I can't digest cow's milk.

I miss carrots
fresh mushrooms
lettuce
and—for goodness sake—zucchini
    which I swore off
    after Amy grew
    four plants of it last year
    on a whim.

We actually used the whopper zuc

as a bat
and played whiffleball
for three hours with Carole.

One of the best times I can remember.

So I figured out why
there's a one-holer out back.

My indoor toilet clogged on day three.

When I went outside and found roots
grappling with the pipe
emerging from the Hovel,
I backed away.

One thing I learned
from last year's geology dig
in Mammoth—
compost toilets are easy.
Throw a little scrub and dirt
on top of your ahems
and voilà—
very little stink.

The outhouse hasn't been used in decades,
dry as coprolite.

So the only thing upset
by my new process
is Grandfather Lizard
who lives below the hole.

Nasty shock for him this afternoon,
after that can of refried beans
got through me.

“So where do you come from, Tilly?
I mean, before here?”

The counter of the Mercantile is sticky
and I head around the back
to grab a cloth.

Tilly is sweaty
in her red-flowered tent of a dress,
cleaning up around the Crock-Pot.

I wipe all the way to the end near the restroom
before I realize she hasn’t answered.

From the end of the counter
I ask her rounded back,
“Tilly? Where did you live before this?”

She is still wiping the same spot.

Finally she takes the Crock-Pot
by the cracked handle,

dragging it into the double sink,
ka-BANG.

"Gonna need a good thoak," she says to it.

I know she heard me.
I decide to leave.

“Desert people’re different,” Milo grunts,
shifting a pail of glaze.

I move another pail for him,
the slosh delicately decorating my foot.

Milo straightens
and looks at me.

“You ask a direct question in the desert,
you are liable to get silence.
After a few months,
you talk about the weather forecast,
they’ll tell you their life story.
Patience.
The desert doesn’t trust outsiders
right away,
Vera.”

I toss my hands in the air.
“But I didn’t even ask anything really *personal*!”

Why does my voice squeak
when I'm frustrated?

A slight smile creases
Milo's left cheek.
"Not personal to *you* . . ." he says.

“You mark the number off here
and match up the dimensions,” Lon says to me.
“We cross-ref everything.”
He is leaning so his smooth naked deltoid
is next to my cheek.
I get the sudden urge to
lick its warm surface,
and pull back from him,
flush-faced.
What the hell, Vera?

He looks down at me.
“Make sense?” he asks,
crow’s-feet appearing with his
half-smile.

I nod.
It’s certainly not what my once best friend Rob
would have called “rocket surgery”—
a third grader could do it.
But Lon’s very serious about this

and my first day
I'd better act as if
it's of
deadly importance.

“So why are you suddenly
here in Garrett?” Lon asks curiously.
“Not that it’s at all bad you’re here,” he adds,
smiling slightly.

I return the smile,
    half pleased
    half concocting what to say.

“Taking some summertime
away from home,”
is what I come up with.

It’s the closest truth I have said
out loud
since I evacuated the coast.

And although I have been hurt
no one has asked me
anything about myself,
I am uncomfortable stating the reason I left.

Do I even know the reason I left?

Lon nods,
and his eyes hold sympathy
which I think I like.

"Yuh," he says,
rubbing his scalp with fingertips.
"Home is sometimes not."

I think about that a long time
after he leaves me
to my calculations.

Walking idly back to the Hovel
I pick up an old trowel
beside my trail.

Practicing trowel flips in the air,
I laugh as I get it right,
catching it by the handle.

Startled a little by my happy voice.
Sheepish.
Desert quiet makes me wary of
personal sound.
Even a fart echoes a long way
'round these parts.

Flipping the trowel
I wonder about using it,
growing something.

Maybe not zucchini.

But Wendy,

from last summer's geo dig,
sent me a paper packet
of her special
eeeenormous
sunflower seeds.
I brought them here
just because they were from Wendy.
They're in a drawer in
the Hovel's kitchen.
Tilly said that woman Pearl
gardens here.
I could ask her what to do.

And it's a strong digging trowel.

Second day on the job for Lon,
by myself in the trailer.

From outside,
Lon sticks his head sideways into the trailer
eyebrows raised.

"Got your hikers on?" he asks.

I pick up my left foot to indicate boots.

"Good."
He disappears,
but his hand is left inside,
finger beckoning me.

Trying to decide
if I am grumpy about being ordered around
without explanation,
I clomp down the metal steps.

Lon grins,

creasing his cheek in that handsome way
that might have made a dimple on a plump face,
and I relent.

“I thought I’d show you some more of
Secondary Packaging’s operation,” he says,
and when he places his hand
lightly on my shoulder
to guide me forward,
I find it friendly and warm.

We walk side by side on the trail.
Though it makes me feel like
    I’m back in middle school,
I like that we walk in step,
left foot and right foot.

The first metal building has been insulated,
that pink fiberglass stuff
just nail-gunned to the inner wood frame.

"Cooler in here," I say in my brilliance.

"Yuh," agrees Lon.
"Got to keep the valuables cool.
Actually, we have AC on generator
if we need it."

"Valuables?" I ask.

He smiles and I can tell
he has been waiting for me to ask
what the product is.

He reaches into an open crate
and takes out a partially wrapped
piece of pottery,
black and red geometries on its surface
in a storm of what looks like

insect elbows and triangular hats.

I wish I could touch the smooth surface.
“Wow,” I say—
    such intellect.

“Hopi,” he says proudly.

“Is that what tribe you are?” I ask,
and then feel pretty dumb,
    white American style,
like when I meet an Asian and have no idea
whether they are
Korean or
Japanese or
Filipino.

Lon is tracing the red pattern
lightly with a forefinger.
“Half,” he says.

He puts the pot back into the crate.
He doesn't say what
his other half is.

“Why is it called ‘Secondary Packaging’?” I ask
as we go through the next metal shed,
the storage and mailing facility.

It’s a pretty slick operation,
        “Oh wow!” I say again—
                where is my vocabulary?
with professional scales
and stacks of boxes and crates
and a metal strapping machine.

Lon starts leading me out.
“Because we get items in one package,
open it
and then repackage each item
for a specific customer.
Secondary packaging.”

Obviously.
I feel a little impatient.
“Yes, but *why*?
Why isn’t the item sent

to the specific customer
at the start?"

Lon's hand on my shoulder
is now propelling me
out into sunlight.

"Good business," he says with a grin.
"We can charge the customer more
to package it better
a second time."

I am still confused
about this business—
    is it all artifacts?
    where do the "items" come from?
    who is buying it?
But Lon has started talking to Andrew
and he turns to ask if it's okay
if I find my own way back
"So you can finish your day sheets."

Um, yuh.

Dismissed.

The trailer is frickin' hot
and I am *not* going to be here
long enough
to bother turning on the little air conditioner.

I buzz through my numbers
wondering
now,
about prices.

I work on invoices
intake numbers
shipment numbers
quantity
and price of packaging.
But not
the price of the "item" itself.

Lon seemed a bit secretive.
Handsome.
Elusive.

Jiggling my left knee
I scan the sheets,
but honestly,
it's boring
and I decide
I'm not interested enough
to keep investigating
and stay
in this
soup can.

I don't know
when Lon is coming back.

Leaving,
the waves off the gravel
are hotter than
the Airstream was,
and I think about
Carole's homemade chilled gazpacho
and the price of pottery.

Feeling a little discouraged
at the desolation
here in Garrett.

What geology major wouldn't love
an old mining town?

But the only things I found
on my rock hunt this morning were
dust
and
bull quartz.

Not just bull quartz,
iron-stained bull quartz—

so named by the miners
because
gold can be found in some quartz,
but not this kind.

This kind of quartz is everywhere

and has
no value.

Bullshit quartz.

My old friend Tanya would have
laughed out loud at that.

Tanya would have laughed at Garrett.
She would have said
"No shopping?"
in a husky incredulous voice.

But she turned into a kind of
bullshit quartz friend,
anyway.

My first earnings from Lon,
I decide I can go
into Dempsey's junk shop with purpose
    instead of skulking around
    knowing I won't buy anything.

When I don't have a job
I don't spend money.

I'm actually kind of
a miser.

But Lon wasn't kidding.

He pays well.

So I am on a shopping mission,
though what I want
won't put a dent
in the cash Lon gave me.

I am pretty sure there are no lights
in this building.
At least, Demps never has them on.
Last week I heard him yell at a rock hound
who bumped into an empty seed rack
"You dent that, you buy it!"

I want a potato masher.
Love mashed potatoes,
even in this heat,
and I am tired of unbending
the tines of my assigned mashing fork.

So. Find a potato masher in the practically dark.

Ceramic swan.
Rifle barrel without the stock.
Black Remette manual typewriter.
A box of . . .
    held up to the window gleam,
a sealed box of condoms.
    Now I am giggling,

most disconcerting.
Coffee percolator.
Cow liniment, rancid.

And then,
a potato masher.

And next to it
the old wooden drawer.
Filled with three hundred postcards.

I tuck both under my arm
and head to the back
to barter.

They sit
on the dresser
in my bedroom,
still stacked upright
in their wooden drawer.

Unlooked through.

Patient
for the right moment.

Sometimes I ruffle
the postcard edges as I walk by to the bathroom.

But I haven't lifted one
out.

In my tank and boxers,
morning hair in tangles,
I stand in front of the dresser,
hand hovering over
the postcards,
feeling for the right one.

My heart is racing
as I pluck one with my fingertips.

"Masai Man"
darkly oiled
and in command of the photograph,
his African lips carved
in sensual lines.

So similar to Lon's mouth.

I tack it with a wire brad
to the wall
beside my bed.

And once I bring them to the bed,
I begin looking
through postcards in a fever—
    Scottish castle
    Icelandic lake
    the Berlin Wall
laughing to find
most are blank,
never sent.

Just like the Moth.
The airline attendant who never
    took her own photographs,
but bought postcards
to mark her global flights.
The airline attendant who never
    sent the postcards to her daughters,
but brought them back
to show off where she'd been.

I sit on the edge of the sheet
    with the embroidered *A*,
deciding to turn on my cell.

Just to look.

Five messages.

All from Carole.

Why the fuck can't my sister leave me alone?
I told Carole I was out of there,
taking back what was left of me,
going to find a place
where I can be who I am
without struggling
to prove I have something of value to share
every time I open my damn mouth.

I told her I was fine.

And she keeps fucking calling.

I jab the button to turn the phone back off,
tuck *A* under the mattress end,
throw shorts over the boxers
and Teva my feet
for an anger-fueled trek in the hills.

Sheeooot.
It's hot.

Really *really* hot like I-did-not-bring-water-what-an-idiot hot.

I am way the hell out to the east of the dunes,
wearing Tevas
to better allow granite rubble
to batter my soles.

I do not have a hat.
I do not have sunscreen.

I am suddenly too fried to think about Carole,
so I stop being mad.

I am turning around.

Who's that?

Who's that lithe girl in jeans standing on that
back dune?
Long dark hair?

The hair on my forearms stands up.

It can't be.

It can't be.

Her arm is up to ward off the low sun.
Too far to see features.

It can't be.

Amy is dead.

The wind is kicking up
as I start off-trail
toward the backlit figure.

And I think about sidewinders
and dunes
and dehydration,

and the windstorm quickly gets more fierce,
whipping particles in dust devils.

Shuttering down my lashes,
I can't see much in that direction anymore.

It can't have been her.

And I need to get my ass
out of this sandstorm
and back to town
pronto.

“Well, you shouldn’t go out in it.”
Milo is stirring glaze with a whisk,
bending over the bucket
like a beach ball witch.
“Bad shit in that wind.”

I’ve never noticed that the glazing room
is completely sealed
apparently insulated
because we can’t hear the wind
other than a high-pitched *fffff*.

I lean back on the counter,
knowing I’ll have clay dust
on my ass,
watching Milo work.
The glaze is smooth slop,
light teal pancake batter.

“Why did you come to a
place of bad shit in the wind, Milo?”

Banging the whisk clean,
he laughs like a murder of crows.

His eyebrows stick out from his face
farther than his nose.

"Love," he says with a shrug and a
slightly wicked grin.

Too quiet in here,
even with Lon on the other side
of the table.

The trailer is stuffy
despite the AC.

Irritable with the mindlessness
of this numbers work,
my brain jumps inexplicably to the Moth
and where she might be
at this moment,
and then I remember I don't care
and go back to the numbers work,
which makes me
irritable with the mindless—

"Nice to have company," Lon says to me.
He stretches,
cracking his upper back,
elbows almost touching the little cabinets
above his seat.

He is smiling at his scripted digits.
"It's so cool to me,
thinking about a piece of Hopi pottery
from here
flying off to live somewhere else on the planet.
Like sending bits of family
out to make connections,
you know?"

Is Lon for real?
Trying to impress me?
I think he's stretching things a bit.

My mother is family
and she goes out into the world.

But that's not me
making a connection.

That's just her.
Gone.

I feel salt-encrusted,
grainy,
grumpy.

Before I jump in the shower
I choose a postcard.

"Butterflies—Rhodes"

Gaudy red underwings
with striped black-and-white uppers.

I am smirking,
remembering how
the Moth
first earned her name.

When Amy was five,
our mother came home
after a long jaunt
    in South America,
tripped eloquently out of the taxi

and hugged the three of us
on the front steps.

She wore a silk butterfly clip
in her hair,
winged on springs
to shiver as she moved.

Amy,
perched carefully in
silk-jacketed arms,
asked
"Why are you wearing the moth
on your head?"

At seven years old
I could tell our mother was
very
irritated
by this.

"It's a *butterfly*,"

she responded with acid.
"Handmade by
an accomplished artist in Argentina."

Amy considered carefully,
craning to look at the fake insect
from all perspectives.

Finally
she shook her head.

"Moth," Amy stated firmly.

Later that same year,
the Moth swept home from Belize
fired our housekeeper
and left again,
after stating that Carole,
    at thirteen years old,
could certainly run the home.

And 'Roley did that,
managing money and clothing and food
with an iron hand
while the Moth
flitted about the planet.

This summer,
now that she's twenty-two,
Carole can relax a bit
with Amy and I gone.

Hiking out just east of Garrett
into sunrise
with a rock hammer
and collecting sack.

Lots of shattered rock out here
chattering behind my boots
on the slope.

I can see the direction I'm going
is not looking promising
for unusual rocks,
but I feel ornery
and press forward,
slithering on unstable footing.

A beetle runs under schist.

Seed fluff wafts over the ground
on indiscernible air currents.

Small wiry plants

grip crevices,
scattered with tiny yellow blooms
that invite me to crouch.

Red ants forage with vicious jaws,
and I decide not to sit.

When I swig from my water bottle
I miss,
    dowsing my face,
and suddenly I hear
my once-friend Rob laughing
like he did at a party our freshman year
when I sloshed my beer,
    a total newbie.

"Like mother,
like daughter!" he crowed.

I remember staring at Rob in shock.

"C'mon," he laughed,

hands gesturing,
"I've known you forever.
You think I haven't seen your mom
slurp out of that flask?"

In the desert of minuscule bugs and plants,
I stand
and pour water over my head,
letting it drain off,
letting it nurture
whoever scrapes a living
under my feet.

I'm still in the trailer, finishing work.
They're all hanging around
a small fire
built inside a mine bucket,
clinking beer bottles:
Andrew, Wind Dog, Dakota, and Hoben.

They're giving Wind Dog shit
about his name,
saying it means dog farts—
    I'm sure he's never heard that one before.
Wind Dog shoves their chests
good-naturedly.
Dakota is stumbling a bit.
This is all on page three of the well-known
  manual
What to Do When You Are Boys with Beer.

I finish the last package
on my day's list
and step out of the Airstream
into fresher evening,

the familiar crunch underfoot.
Lon is sitting in a splitting lawn chair
cradling a bottle of water,
beaming gently at his posse
like an uncle.

"Want a beer, Vera?" He gestures to the ice tub.
I shake my head.
He still hasn't looked at me.

"Why aren't you joining them?" I ask.

"I never drink." His words are clipped.
"Too many alcoholics in the family."

And then the sharp smile comes out,
a winking satellite
against darkening sky.

I turn on my phone
and stare at it.

Six messages.

Irresponsible muscular impulses
press the call-in button
and push the phone to my ear
to hear my older sister
'Roley's familiar voice.
"Vera, *please* just let me know
where you are,
that you're okay—"

Responsible muscular impulses
take over,
press 7 for delete,
and my lacrimal ducts
swallow
excess eye fluid in one gulp.

Teapots are the hardest.
Delicate handle,
perfectly edged spout,
requiring miles of Bubble Wrap
and a box filled 60 percent with styro-flo pack.

I tried to convince Milo
to save
by going smaller.

"I've got the ratio right, Veer.
Do it my way."

He says this patiently,
and I don't get pissy,
which is astonishing all on its own.

When has anyone ever dealt with me so deftly?

Most of the time I feel like a corkscrew burr,
ready to stab with impatience
at any odd angle.

But Milo does something differently.
He's made differently.

It certainly isn't

me

changing my burr-osity.

Milo asked
casually
about my family
this afternoon,
as we stood in the almost-cool doorway
of the glazing shed.

The answer
"My older sister works,
my mother's off on a trip"
didn't appease a thing
and I knew it.

Do I want him to ask more?

He didn't.
He didn't say "What about the dead sister?"
because he doesn't know
because I haven't told anyone.

Because that just opens up the whole dirty
midden
and the digging don't stop
till somebody's crying.

Amy started the writing-on-the-beloved-
postcards
thing.

One evening
Carole and I walked in the door
at the same time,
and on the table was
a postcard of a fluffy kitten with a bright pink
background
stating "I miss you!"
Gag.

Who knows where the Moth got it,
but we had all seen it before
when we snuck a peek through the stash of
cards
and laughed about it.

When 'Roley turned it over,
Amy's writing stated,

Out with Tricia at Denny's,
then homework at her house,
invited to stay overnight,
so much love!

—which is how the Moth signed anything to us.

Amy never did homework unless
Carole or I
stood over her.

And she constantly complained
that Tricia's house
smelled like cauliflower,
something we never cooked at home
because Amy got nauseous.

We were so impressed by Amy's
audacity,
writing on a precious postcard,
that we ignored
the lies.

She was heading out to party.
We both assumed that.
And said nothing.

But Amy did start the fun
of finally using the Moth's postcards.

Carole's notes on the postcards had purpose
and bossiness.

But they were still entertaining.

"Alaska—King Crab Chowder Recipe"
had a note to me that it was my turn
to make everyone dinner.

I actually made the recipe,
though only Amy and I ate it.
Carole doesn't eat seafood.
Too close to her work in marine biology.

"Wherever You Go There Is a Lovely View in
Grenada"
had a nasty message for Amy
to clean her room
or we would have to distribute gas masks.

"England—The Queen Outside"

showed the stiff monarch riding a horse and
saluting the camera,
and Carole's note read

THE MOTH ARRIVES IN TWO WEEKS.
PREPARE THYSELVES.

But it was a false alarm, as usual.
The Moth rarely comes home
when she says she will.

One night at two a.m.
I investigated a noise in the kitchen.

Amy was eating thick Cheez Whiz on bread,
    not exactly fodder for an athlete,
but what made me stare
was dark eyeliner
smeared around her eyes.

None of us has ever worn makeup.

"What's *that* shit?" I said,
    flicking my hand at her.

"Chizwhz," Amy mumbled
with her mouth full,
deliberately misunderstanding.

A large burp escaped as she finished eating,
and fumes of liquor
expanded into the room.

“’Mgoing to bed, swim practice in the morning,”
she gurgled,
placing her plate by the sink
and walking out with a slight list.

“It *is* morning,” I said softly,
in a sudden swell of sorrow.

Where is the Moth
when you need one?

Sitting on the back porch
in the shade
  already deadly
at this dawn-ish hour
without a glass of water at hand.
Staring.

The problem with living alone
is that all the time you normally spend
conversing
is now just you and your thoughts.

What is Carole doing right now?
Already had her tea and bagel from Lott's Bakery
and is stepping primly aboard
Henley Queen
to stick her head up her ass with
oceanographic research.

What's the Moth doing right now?
Buenos Aires, last we knew.
Probably perfectly made up and coiffed,

impeccable linen trousers,
already tipping back a sip or two or three,
that vague look of
    "I'm here and beautiful and that's enough."

What is Amy do—
Oh.
Right.
Dead.

It is seven thirty a.m.
Not a slip of wind.

I wearily go in for my mug
and without thinking
pluck a postcard from
right up near the front.

A tiny conifer clinging to crumbling rock face,
with a massive stone block building
in the distance
squatting impossibly
on towering conglomerate rock.

"Agiou Nikolaou Anapafsa Monastery—
Meteora, Greece"

The building imposing,
demanding.

But all I see
is the little pine tree.

I remember
the scent of sun-warmed pine needles.
Pine needles and the Moth's ringed fingers
clamped painfully with mine and Carole crying
  and crying and crying and crying
till I wanted to slap her.
It wasn't helping,
all the crying.

It just upset everyone else
at the funeral
trying to comfort us.
Well, comfort *Carole*.
Because she was crying so hard.

I got pissed off that she was so irresponsible
and had to leave the building.
Stomped out the side door,
across the sea-misted lot
and past the first few protected pines
to the smallest tree.

I spent at least twenty minutes out there,
my back on its narrow uncomfortable trunk,
swearing at my big sister Carole
    for working incessantly
    instead of paying attention to Amy.

And as I sat there,
the Moth snuck out the same side door,
voluminous purse in hand,
shakily smoothing her peach blazer.
The taxi arrived in less than a minute.

So I leaned on my pine tree a bit longer,
swearing at the Moth for not staying
    for the entire funeral of her youngest
      daughter—
            well, to hell with that,
swearing at the Moth for being unavailable,
  period.
Ever.

Eventually I wiped my eyes to go back in,
face the final dirge.
I felt the telltale ick of sap
bleeding through
the back of Amy's favorite blue shirt.

I threw it away after.
Part of the funereal process.

I never got around to
swearing at Amy for dying,
but I'll bet if I run into the smell
of solarized
pine pitch
again
I'll swear at her, too.

A few weeks after the funeral
I chose the postcard from the Moth's stash
very carefully.

"The Dead Sea—
Lowest Point on Earth"

CAROLE,

I AM TAKING OFF FOR A WHILE. I'VE
GOT SOME MONEY AND I'LL FIND A JOB
SOMEWHERE. YOU ARE VERY BUSY WITH
WORK, AND YOU'LL HAVE LESS TO DEAL
WITH WHEN I'M GONE.

—VERA

Laundry.
Hand-washing is not a big deal
when I wear the same thing
almost every day.

Not like loads to go in the washer
and into the dryer
and then to be folded.
I hate that.

Here it's just desert laundry:
unders
bra
T-shirt
shorts.

I have started a habit
of doing them
every morning,
rotating two sets.

They never really smell
clean.
But since local grime attaches
in three minutes outside,
doesn't matter.

We are panting,
unloading a bisque load
from the kiln.

Just a slight breeze
so far,
coming off the range.

"How can the air here
not smell like something?" I ask.

Milo stares at me blankly.
"Too hot?" he suggests.

I gesture up the slope.
"Scrub, dust, carcass, something—
something must have a smell."

We keep unloading
fragile pots
ahead of the coming storm.

Dempsey limps by
with two fingers raised in greeting to Milo,
and the rising gusts
wrap my face
with his body odor.

I reel back.

"There it is." Milo laughs.
"*That* smells like something!"

Heading down from Milo's
I see Pearl
puttering with a planter in the alley
wearing inexplicably white sneakers.

She lifts her head to see me,
pure white curls bobbling
under the brim
of her Aussie sun hat.

"Hey there, Vera," she says
    in a half-whisper,
    a bit Marilyn Monroe
    but not as affected.

"Hi, Pearl!" I say as softly,
stepping cautiously into the alley,
thinking she might skitter away.
"I wanted to—
Can I see how you garden?"

The resulting smile turns Pearl into a cherub,

and she minces toward me,
free hand outstretched.

Is she going to take my hand like a child?

"You want to start one at your place?
I got plenty of seeds. . . ."

When I don't take her hand, she beckons with it
and I follow her
through the gate,
noticing her sneakers
are neatly coated with
white paint.

Eden enclosed.
Vegetation lounges luxuriantly,
topping the brick walls,
scrambling across crumbled schist paths,
twenty by twenty feet of
peppers, tomatoes, lettuce, grapes,
herbs, rampantly flowering runner bean,
and an enormous fig tree,
    alternately smooth and knobbly limbed.

Heaven.
Or at least a damp slice of heaven
here in Garrett.

Pearl introduces me to each plant
by name
including something viny I do not recognize
    called Leticia.
She beams at me and whispers,
"Kiwi!"

"Kiwi?" I practically shout.

In the desert?
"Is Leticia the variety of Kiwi?"

She shakes her head,
eyes closed in rapture.
"Donald named her."

Is that her husband? Was that her husband?

I kneel and dig two fingers into the soil.
Soft, dark, loamy earth.
She opens her eyes to watch,
pleased and nodding.
"Fortuna the Hen helps. And my worms."

Pearl plucks my T-shirt sleeve,
cocking her head so curls bounce.
"Would you like to see the seed bunker?"

I stumble toward the Hovel
two hours later,
laden with a bucket of starting mix,
overwhelmed with the shift
    from the luscious green growth of
    Pearl's garden
    to
    the dead dry snarls of wind
    coming up for the evening.

I spin internally
with the dust whirls on the road,
still hearing Pearl's sotto voice
as she patted seed packets
snug in the drawers of her "bunker,"
telling me how deeply
    to plant my sunflowers from Wendy,
and how talking out loud
is good for their cell structures.

Well, shit.

Talking out loud to plants is no different
than
talking out loud to the walls.

I'll try it.

I dump my dinner dishwashing water
onto the dirt out back,
and dig some starting mix in.
A little dry
but I keep watering.

Dimpling dirt with my forefinger,
dropping a striped seed in
sprinkling mix over,
water water drippling,
repeat,
rinse,
repeat,
rinse,
repeat.

I am punchy with glee
that I will have
towering
fat-faced flowers
tracking the desert sun.

Lon and I
are taking a water break outside
on the shady side of the trailer
when I ask if he has
a big family.

"A sister.
She's twelve."
Lon sighs,
his mouth dropped on the edges.

As soon as I asked the question
I realized I was on dangerous ground.
I swipe at my forehead with my T-shirt sleeve,
which comes away
damp-smeared the color of underdone toast.

I don't want him
to ask me
about *my* sister.

But he isn't focusing on me

at all.

"She's got some disabilities, yuh?
She needs taking care of."
Lon squints out past the immediate
group of trucks
into the rough ridges
and maybe farther
to the Rez
beyond.

"My uncle Vel takes care of her now, mostly.
My mom drinks a lot," he adds,
flat and thin
like a flake of obsidian.

I connect a few things.

"While she was pregnant?" I ask.

He nods
once
sharply.

The drawer is in front of me on the counter
while I eat
a block of iceberg lettuce
for dinner.

The dingy postcard that emerges is
"Olympic Flame"
with a group of people
standing in choreographed positions
around
a young girl in an embroidered dress
    receiving the torch.

I am amazed to find
her face looks like mine,
heart-shaped
and responsible.

I didn't graduate.
I mean, I didn't *go* to graduation.
It was right before the funeral

and I was tired of sad sympathy.

I still had a diploma mailed to me.
Who needed pomp,
given the circumstances?

CAROLE,

I'VE GRADUATED TO NOWHEREVILLE. GOT A JOB, PLACE TO LIVE, PRETTY COUNTRY, NICE FOLKS, GROWING A GARDEN. HOPE YOUR BOAT IS STILL AFLOAT.

—VERA

Before I can think,
I write in the address.

Before I can act on it,

I tuck the postcard
into the folder with my cash,
re-stashing it
under the loose
bathroom floorboards.

I'm in the Mercantile
for just about seven seconds
and Tilly fluffs my head,
cackling
"Wiry head of hair, huh, girl?"

My arm goes up to ward off
such a personal touch,
and I'm almost blown backward
by bourbon fumes.

My hair is probably straightened.

"Yowza, woman," I say,
grabbing the bottle from the counter
to look.
"Do you even know
what alcohol can do to you?
They've proven it kills brain cells."

Tilly moves with sudden grace,

swiping the bottle
out of my hand.

"You don't know everything, girl,"
she growls.
"Who made you the drink polithe?"

I whirl and slam out the door.

"I know alcohol can kill you,
bitch,"
I mutter
when I'm halfway across the road,

then through anger
swells that sorry feeling.

Like when you have the flu
and your body flashes
hot and cold.

Dumb death.

People die
being dumb
every day.

Like in the old
Ghost and Mrs. Muir movie
  where this hale cantankerous sea captain
  became a ghost because
  he left the gas heater on
  in his bedroom,
  fell asleep,
  and *pffft*—asphyxiated.

  Didn't have the spiritual spunk
  to die properly at sea.

Not all deaths are
noble or

horrific or
meaningful.

Not even when they die at sea.

Amy was a really freaky great swimmer.

Carole always said
Amy realized the Moth wouldn't be around
much
so she gathered
water from the womb
as she was born
and took it with her into life.

She became California champion
in 5K ocean swimming at age thirteen.

U.S. champion in the 10K this year,
the day after her fifteenth birthday.

In July, this month,
Amy was going to travel to the
FINA World Open Water Swimming
Championships
in China.

Favored to win the women's 10K.
Qualify for the Olympics.

But on June third,
she went to a midnight beach party.

One of the biggest fights ever with Carole.

At the house
I had met two of Amy's latest
rather older
"friends"
who made me prickly and fearful—
    they were out-of-Amy's-league sketchy.
I asked around,
and people said they were dropouts,
into hard-core drinking
and maybe some other shit.

I was responsible
    as usual
bringing up my findings
with my older sister
so we could decide how to handle it.

Except Carole told me
I was overreacting.

"Everyone parties a little, Vera," she said,
shaking water from the colander
full of rice noodles.

Then she swiveled her head
through the steam
like some practiced prehistoric swamp
  vertebrate.
"Well, everyone except you.
But just because *you* don't party
doesn't mean it's some crime or something."

I blew a gasket.
"What the fuck are you talking about, 'Roley?
You never party!
You never even relax
or get your head out of your research
to have any idea who these people are
but I've seen them
talked to them
and Amy is fifteen years old!"

I remember colander vapors
whooshing up the sides of her face
from the tsunami of my anger.

Lon and I are chilling
    or trying to
    in this heat
under the awning of the Airstream,
watching Dakota and Hoben
scuffle in a patch of shade.

Dakota is bigger
and keeps trying to snag Hoben's leg
as he dances by.
They are laughing
and finally get to pummeling each other
when Lon speaks.

"These guys are my family," he says
in a low solemn voice.
"It was good to get off the Rez,
and be able to bring them
with me
to start this company."

He takes a swig of his Fresca,

Adam's apple dipping smoothly.
Blech, I think at the soda,
Beautiful, I think at Lon's throat.
And I like that Lon is telling me
things that are personal.

"Family of any kind is the most
important thing," he says,
sounding like a damn commercial.
"Family is home,"
he states,
and cheers as
Hoben trips Dakota to the ground.

As I tilt back my water bottle,
a rivulet runs from my chin.

I don't know that I agree with Lon.

Crunching my way back to the Hovel.

I miss Rob.

I miss Tanya, too.

Or,
maybe I don't.

For being my best friends since just about
  forever
they stabbed me pretty hard.

We were three together
in everything since third grade,
and suddenly at the end of our senior year
they're in love?
Running off to Spain for the summer
    the two of them,
and didn't even tell me
they'd gotten the plane tickets

till the week before final exams.
Just before Amy disappeared.

I'm whining.
Justified whining.

Because
it's not like
I wanted to date Rob.

But they shouldn't date each other, either.

Isn't that some sort of code with
best friends?

It's my hips, I bet.

I have these hips,
swingin'-wide country-style hips.

Tanya has that straight-sided,
bubble-butted
African-American thing going
that she always hated

but Rob apparently loves it.

I never thought of Tan from his side before.

That crème chocolat skin
the long thighs
the small upstanding—

okay I'm done.

Obviously
Rob and Tanya
have moved on.

Closing the door of the outhouse
I unzip,
reveling in my mood,
draping dark heat,
and the slight stink.

And look at me,
sitting on a desert shit hole.

Obviously
I have moved on
to a new place
too.

When I reemerge

to sharp sunlight
and fresher air,
I decide
to go see what Milo's up to.

I don't know why I didn't ask Milo first.
He'd probably like to teach me.

He's not here,
and I for some reason need to do this now,
right now.
I've watched him eight million times—
how hard could it be?

He just slams the ball of clay
on the center of the wheel,
wraps his hands around,
caresses it into a smooth breast shape,
down into the middle,
out and up,
and a mug forms,
or a bowl,
or a vase
with an out-turned delicate pouting lip.

And here I have a misshapen revolving bulk
nowhere near the center of the wheel,

and suddenly I am screaming,
slamming it with my fist,
blops of slip flying around me
off the wheel head
    as it spins at top speed,
and I don't stop
till there is little mass left
and my fist scrapes grit,
cutting the side of my palm.

One sharp shriek of pain
and I turn off the wheel,
panting,
watching the thin stripe of blood
drip to the brown slurry of mud.

I clean everything
and hurry down to the Hovel,
ashamed.

This postcard seems extra shiny.
Like you can't quite
trust it.

"Flamingos—San Diego Zoo—California"

How screwy is a flamingo?

Upside-down beak hinge,
whacked-out color,
and so many tacky plastic birds around
it's hard to know
when the thing is actually real.

One windy spring evening
the Moth arrived home
for a surprise visit.

I had her to myself a bit
with Amy partying
and

Carole working.

The Moth patted me on the wrist
and beckoned me to sit with her
in the porch swing.

I was thrilled and worried,
lining up the important things
I needed to talk
to my mother about
    Carole never listening to me
    Amy's sketchy new friends
    the weird vibe from Rob and Tanya,
but I wasn't sure the Moth was really
the person
to ask anyway
and I sat with my hands in my lap.

The Moth sat under
the soft yellow lantern,
flicking her hair off her forehead,

and proceeded to regale me
with stories of some man in Lucerne,
complete with giggles
and a light "Oh my, it was grand!"

Then her eyes closed
    to show perfect eyeliner
and she begged in a little girl voice for
four ibuprofen.
"My headache is simply blistering."

When I came back and sat with her,
she swallowed the pills,
pronounced she was
utterly exhausted,
blew me a kiss
and went in to bed.

I was left to pendulum
slightly unbalanced

by the lack of weight
on her end
of the swing.

She left the next morning.

So Rob leaves me to be with Tanya
and Tanya leaves me to be with Rob
and Amy leaves me to be the youngest again
and Carole is cold as her ocean
and the Moth is never around
even when you leave the light on.

Suck it up, girl.

You're on your own.

The cardboard can says
BARGAIN TIME LEMONADE,
made of corn products
and some probably genetically engineered
citric acid.

But it's tart
and thirst-quenching
with four mini ice cubes from the teensy freezer.

Tart helps
when I'm angry.

And I'm angry a lot of the time.

Even as I sit on the porch
in stillness of failing sunbeams,
a breeze tossing the scrub leaves
over my bare feet,
I am angry.

In general.

At what?

Life is pretty good here in the desert.

All we know
is what her new pals
    Drake and Bev
told the police.

They never came to tell us themselves.

After the beach bonfire and boozing,
Tim challenged Amy—
    Amy!—
to a swimming race out to the buoy
and back.

I can see her,
laughing at Tim,
who is a good athlete, but no ocean swimmer.

I can see Amy tossing that hair,
winding it quickly into a knot,
    even drunk,
throwing off clothing
as she sprinted

easily
into the chill water.

Drake and Tim
tumbled in after her,
and Tim apparently
made it to the buoy.
Then he started shouting to shore
that he couldn't see Amy.

She was way ahead of him
and way faster.

For two hours her friends decided
she was hiding in the dunes,
playing games.

The Coast Guard divers combed the kelp beds,
but they never found her body
and they called off
the surrounding search
after a week.

That first week
I was on the beach
all day
accompanied by the intermittent chop
    of helicopter blades,
hiking south with the swell,
hoping to find her,
terrified to find her,
    and I walked in the door each night,
desperate for Amy to be sitting at our table
    eating microwaved nachos.

I badgered the Coast Guard mercilessly.
I got the spokesperson's phone number,
calling every three hours.

The Moth said to me repeatedly
"We need to let them do their job,"
and sat
dry-eyed
flipping *Ultimate Travel*,

slipping sips from her flask.

After the officials called it off,
I walked the beach another week,
sunscalded,
heels cracking
from drying saline sands.

I catch him leaving the trailer.
"Lon," I call,
and when I run a bit and meet him
I can tell
he's distracted and serious.

"Morning, what do you need?"

Already telling me I am an imposition.

In a flare of temper,
I ask anyway.

"Just wanting to know more about the business.
I have a couple questions,
you know,
but hey, when you have time—"

"What questions?" he interrupts sharply.

And now I am waving my hands
with no purpose

trying to find words.
Lon doesn't seem very friendly today,
slick with a fierce intensity
new to me.
Obviously this is not a good time to ask.

"Ask now, or do it later, Vera."

"I, uh, wanted to know
how you price things?
Like the items and things?
How much is this stuff we're packaging worth?"

I added that last bit—
    "we're packaging"—
so he could see I'm asking as a team member.
Pretty bright.

His smile is short and appeasing.
"Oh, that's a need-to-know thing.
For the privacy of the client,
the collector,

only a few of us know pricing.
And the items are privately collected,
so the fewer people who handle the items
the better."

Then he waves at the Airstream.
"Go on in," he says.
"Your work is waiting for you."

With a small attempt to smile,
he turns and walks toward his truck.

I hear him mutter a question
starting with "Who?"
and ending with
a short string of swears.

Definitely stressed out
about
something.

I am hopping up and down excited
because I have never
gotten to unload a glaze kiln before.

Milo mans the lever
and the door swings slowly wide
revealing glassy surfaces
brilliant carmine,
metallic russet brown.

"That color," states Milo,
presenting a curvy beet red vase,
"is what reduction firing is all about."

Gorgeous is the only word.

I can't tell if Milo knows
I tried to throw on his wheel,
but neither of us says anything.

We start moving still-warm pottery
from kiln to the rolling cart,

oohing at almost every piece,
touching the belly of each jug,
the flat of every plate.

I tell Milo just a little about Lon.

"Well, he's a handsome one," is all Milo says.

Holding up a midnight blue platter
constellated with white flecks and
  a small red nebula
I grin.
"Not as handsome as this!"

Milo laughs—
what I say is true.

Driving Milo's decrepit pickup
the forty-five minutes
into Barville,
mailing a slew of packaged pottery.

Feeling cramped with so many cars
on the road.

Self-conscious about
hand-trucking the stack of boxes
from the parking lot.

Shocked by the sudden noise of voices
inside the post office
the intrusive friendliness
the smiles
the waves
the pats on the arm for gawdsake.

I am almost panting
with stress

when I get back into the truck.

Squealing my wheels out of town
to the independent desert
like some yokel.

I've only been in Garrett three weeks
and already I feel battered
by Barville's greater
social graces.

I can't believe this postcard is in here
just for geo-me:
"Bending Columns—Staffa, Western Isles"

Tourists climbing on huge basalt pillars,
these rock formations that
only happen in perfect circumstances
of cooling magma.

Last summer I got invited
on a research gig
to the ones in Mammoth,
at Devils Postpile.
Studied decay rate,
    falling columns,
compared to previous years.
Measured the hexagonal tops,
like a bee on honeycomb of black stone.

We camped nearby for three weeks,
and it was so amazing
to be with researchers,

students,
professors,
all interested in the same thing I am,
like relations
in some way.

I met Wendy there,
    a student from Oregon,
    frickin' unbelievable knitter,
and Peg, the camp cook.
We played rummy and sang
"McTavish Is Dead"
over and over,
and laughed till tears ran down our faces.

I was offered a position
on this summer's research gig,
but
Rob and Tanya and I were excited
    I thought
about spending our last summer
together

before leaving for college.
So my invite sat waiting,
Amy died,
Rob and Tanya flew off to Spain.

I did get another invite
and a phone message from Wendy,
"Just come whenever you can."

I never responded.

I'm taking the long path,
meandering,
keeping an eye out
for desert iguanas
    sleek blunt-nosed creatures
and find myself
intersecting paths with
a small woman
in a ranger outfit.

She raises a hand
in a real wave,
not the desert two-finger jobbie.

"Hi! MaryBeth. Rock hunting?" she says.

"Iguana hunting," I say, grinning.

"Oh, aren't they amazing? Love the iguanas.
Oh, hey, don't go out too far,

we're expecting big winds.
I was doing tailing samples,
but I'm not allowed to stay out here
when winds reach over twenty-five miles per
hour."

I am a little lost on this.

"Arsenic," she explains.
"These hills have the highest concentration in
the U.S.
Winds kick in,
all that stuff is in the air—
lung cancer recipe.
Well,
have a good morning with the iguanas!"

I laugh with her
and watch her tiny frame
maneuver with strength

downhill.

An arsenian dust devil whips up to the west.
I start slanting down
toward the Hovel.

I don't miss the Internet
as I lie here on my bed
paperback in hand
ignoring the howl around the north corner.

All the videos
chats
mail
messaging
friends
    everything I thought so important
    in every day of life
everything is carrying on without me.

There are jillions of books
in the shack
in back.
Stacked floor to nail-pokey ceiling.

Right now it's probably three p.m.

Sometimes I am ripped from Arthur C. Clarke
by the spray of sand
fffft-ing under the door,
but I find now and then
I can recognize it and not turn to look

and so I believe
I am comfortable here.

8:45 p.m.

Electricity's out.

Cold turkey chili from the can
with a side of grit.

Not grits.

Grit.

I have never been in anything like this.
I lie on the mattress
in dead blackness,
a damp T-shirt over my mouth and nose
against dust.
Wind shrieks around the cabin,
rattling windows with ferocity.

The oil lamp I found won't stay lit
in the sucking whirl of current
coming through chinks
in the redwood walls.

Torrents of rain suddenly
pummel the roof.
A flash of lightning
shows mud dotting the window
and the room becomes muggy and close.

With a new level on the Beaufort wind scale,
my shovel is rapidly bapping against
the outside wall of my bedroom.

Heart pounding with it,
I suck air through the T-shirt faster,
a little balloon of fabric puffing in and out of my
mouth,
and I start to panic about oxygen,
suddenly thinking of Amy
panicking about oxygen as she goes down,
trying not to take in that mouth of water,
needing to breathe,
needing air
needing—

Was that a voice?

I half sit, clutching the sheet.

Another flash of lightning
and outside the window
an indistinct face,
long dark hair wet-whipped in the wind
hand against the glass pane
mouth open

yelling something something
something
I can't hear.
I yell "Amy?"
Leap from bed,
wrap myself mightily in the sheet,
yank the front door,
race barefoot around to the back.

And struggling to stand up in slick mud,
pelted by painful rain,
I halt at the corner.
No one.
  No footprint.
  No handprint on the mud-splatted window.

I stand hunched against the wind,
wet sheet decoupaged
to my body.

Awake because of silence at three a.m.
The storm is gone.

I had fallen into an exhausted zonk,
my hair still wet,
now dried stuck to my head,
and I am feeling raw-edgy from wrapping naked
in the rough blanket.

The Hovel is an oven.

I try the light,
    blindingly functional,
and go to the postcards.

My right hand picks
"Johann Strauss Monument—Vienna"
Smooth and elegant
clean marble
in a parklike setting.

We got Amy a memorial stone

since there was nothing to bury.

A little stone with her name,
nothing else,
up on the bluff overlooking the ocean.

Carole convinced me.
It seemed like enough.
What does a memorial do, anyway?
It's for the living.
Who probably don't want to go sit next to it
and cry.

Strauss's Monument is
prissily gorgeous
fashionably excessive
wildly expensive—
and for what?
No one who knew him is alive.

Three hundred years from now,
will anyone care who Strauss was?

And certainly no one will care who Amy was.
She wasn't even famous yet.

CAROLE,

WORK IS GOOD, MY BOSS IS FRICKIN' CUTE (!), FASCINATING PEOPLE IN THIS TOWN, AND THE HOT WINDS ARE FEROCIOUS. I SURE MISS THE PACIFIC. AND AMY. THOUGHT I SAW HER THE OTHER DAY, HA-HA!

—VE

My pen runs out when I get to the *R* in *VERA*.

I decide to keep this one
in the money folder,
too.

I tread over to the Mercantile.
The bleary rising sun
illuminates Lon and Hoben
sitting with iced tea
like some painting by Vermeer.

"Aw, Vera."
    Lon tilts his head sympathetically.

Do I look that bad?
I feel that bad.

"Thet down, hawney. I'll gitchyou thome tea."
Tilly hefts herself out of the chair,
bustles to the sink
to rinse out a glass.

"Hard night, wasn't it?" he says to me,
patting the chair next to him.
"The door in Prepackaging was damaged,
    flew open overnight.
We lost a few pieces

during the worst of it."

"I was fine," I mumble,
perching on the hard chair edge.

Behind me,
iced tea gluggling into my glass
makes me feel desperately thirsty
  and unfocused.
When Tilly shuffles to me I practically grab it,
drinking it down in one swoop.

I hand the glass back to her
and wipe my mouth with my knuckles.

"Thanks," I say softly.

Lon rubs my shoulder.
"How about another, Tilly?" he says,
gazing at my face.

She scoots behind the counter again.

Sitting up on the peak,
looking down at the scattered town
covered in sepia dust
like an old photograph.

Not a romantic photograph.
More scraping-the-bean-can
unapologetic
starkness.

A stagnant dust bowl of the Old West,
the sniper of death
picking them off
one by one
till no one is left at all.

They farm this.

They want to be left alone.

I don't understand.
No jobs.

No families.

It's not like anyone is mining now.

What keeps them here?

Six a.m.,
and it's already "hotter 'n Hades,"
    as Dempsey says.

I slide down the gravel slope
between Dempsey's rusting trailer
and an old wood shack,
dust off my scraped hands and stand,
heading past Pearl's.

Every piece of detritus
no matter how small
winds up around her house,
placed just so among succulents
and derelict birdhouses.
I've seen her move a Swanson's
  chicken broth can
three millimeters to the left
during a conversation.

I see the broth can now,
just as she placed it

at the base of the ten-foot wooden stake.
Pearl slung colorful glass bottles at the top
neck-first on nails,
aiming in all directions.

The first thing in her yard to catch daylight.

As I pass,
the screaming morning sun
flares the bottles blue-green-gold
from behind
and I feel tears fill my eyes
for the beauty
in loneliness.

Seedlings!

Seedlings pushing through!

Oh, the perfect two-leafed precious sprouts of
GREEN!

I am jigging in the breeze
as the largest toss their bobbleheads.

A garden.

I have done it—

I have created life
where once there was
none!

Milo went into Barville just to get
baby back ribs
and let it be known
that he makes the most fabulous maple-laced
  bone-sucking sauce
ever.

And I should know.

I had four helpings.

Tilly and Milo and I are sitting together,
out back of his house,
our sticky fingers limp over our knees.

I am burping root beer loudly
when Milo turns to me and says,
"Want me to teach you to throw pots, Veer?"

And I shrug,
flushing.

“If you want,” I say,
and shrug again
looking away.

In the morning I am hunched
over Milo's wheel as it spins,
trying to pressurize the
lump of clay
into being centered.

Ha.

"Now, gently push on the sides
with your hands,
cone up."
Milo gestures with his own hands,
hands that manipulate clay like cream cheese.

We have tried this maneuver
many times.

Milo has been very patient.

I have not.

Eventually,

Milo sighs a bit.
"How about a break?
You did great your first day!"

But if I can't get centered in one hour,
there won't be a
second day.
I am silent.

"Everyone has a hard time starting, Veer,"
he says encouragingly.
"We'll try again another day."

I wash up,
swearing as the soap slips onto the dusty floor.
I am pissy and sheepish,
but manage to say thank you
with a small wave
as I shoulder into the laughing blinding heat.

Dingling through the door chime of the
Mercantile.
Tilly is serving lunch
to a young teen boy and his dad,
rock hounds.

I sit at the other end of the counter
and lift a finger to her.

She lumbers over.
"You here t'eat?"

I look at the bearded man's plate.
Tough morning
unsuccessfully battling clay
and suddenly I'm famished.

"I'll have one of those sandwiches."

The son happily exclaims
he just turned fifteen,

and I grin
as he brandishes his new rock hammer.

I count the cans of Vienna sausages
on the shelf in front of me
till Tilly slaps my plate down.

Half of the sandwich is devoured
before I taste the liverwurst
and actually groan with pleasure.

The boy glances at me.

"Liverwurst!" I say with my mouth full.
"It's been so long!"

Tilly's hands are on her hips,
her mouth in a leer.
"Well, don't that beat all."

The fifteen-year-old is okay-cute,

but I am seventeen and he's fifteen and

he's not

Lon.

I am diligent.
Good with details.
Shaping numbers.

So this job is easy for me.
And only three hours
a few days a week.

It's so easy
that I am a little suspicious
Lon is paying me so much.

Any of the guys could do this.

And a lot of the time I am the only one,
alone in the trailer
with that acerbic scent of Pine-Sol or something.

I work so fast I could do the work in,
seriously?
Forty-five minutes.

Seriously.

But I stay.
Not for the availability of the nasty
boy-infested trailer bathroom.

But because when Lon happens in,
I get a wired thrill
from both
his lean thighs in jeans
and
the swirling cauldron of
    caring and turmoil
that bubbles under his shoulders
as he reaches
in front of me
for the stapler.

I wake up from one of those morning dreams
where you are desperately looking
for a public toilet.
Bursting by the time I hobble
in untied boots
to the already roasting outhouse.

Perched on the wooden seat,
I stop peeing to listen.

Sirens?

Sirens!

I hear them coming down
the back road from Barville,
and by the time
two EMT trucks and two ranger vehicles
wail through,
I have pulled up my jeans,
somehow re-laced boots,
grabbed my bandanna

and am sprinting,
following the vehicle dust clouds,
sprinting
the upslope toward the mine.

Who?

Scrub blurs by,
        part of my running self
                noting that the plants near the trail
                move faster
                than the plants farther away.
My lungs may split
with dryness,
shedding pleural lining
like snakeskin.

I round the bend
dip through the shallow
and the mine entrance
is above on the slope,
EMTs and rangers and Milo's truck there
and Lon and the boys just arriving.

I fly
finding it hard to pull a halt
stretching my hands out to Milo's torso
to slow

and he catches me
putting an arm over my shoulders.

I push out the only word.
"Who?"

Milo is staring through
the hush of the seven a.m. desert
toward the dark mine entrance.

"A boy,
fifteen years old.
He and his father ate lunch
    at the Merc yesterday,"
he says quietly,
as if he is in pain.
"He fell in the mine shaft.
His father called to say he
couldn't get a response,
couldn't reach him at the bottom."

And apparitioning
out of the silken black
come four EMTs,
adjusting the load of boy
strapped to spine board,

the father holding his foot,
weeping.

And suddenly
I am running forward
to meet them,
shouting
"Is he all right?"
like an idiot
because the boy is lifeless,
trickling blood from his mouth,
his sweaty hair plastered
against a face of paste,

and the EMTs slither on schist to the wagon,
sliding him in,
his father clambering after him,
and I find the ranger MaryBeth
by my side
and I say to her
"Can I help?"
    how fucking dumb

knowing I'm asking too late.

MaryBeth gently squeezes my forearm
and says
"I think he's out of our hands now.
We need to let them do their job,"
and immediately
my arm hair stands up,
my throat opens to wail,
accompanied by
the siren of the ambulance
as it hauls downslope
in a practiced
slide.

Lon has come up behind me,
his arms circling,
saying
“Shhh-shhh, Vera,
there’s nothing we can do,”

which only makes me
change tone
to something more ragged
and visceral.
But I feel him holding me up
and a small shred
of comfort
gets through.

Slowly I realize
solid Milo is next to me
as well,

he and Lon focused
on comforting me,

and my outburst shuts off
like a vault door closing.

Crying doesn't help anything.

Afternoon.
I am actually basking in the superheated
Airstream oven,
the sensation of being
fused
sealed
a warm crusting over.

Not doing my work,
though it's sitting there.

Stillness
in the trailer,
in my head.

Until Lon comes tramping in
and kindly says
"You kind of lost it this morning, yuh?"
with a pat on my scorched skin.
"Well, getting back to work
is the best escape."

He bounces lightly down
trailer steps,
missing my muttered comment.

"Fuck you, 'Roley."

After my sunbaked anger-march back to the
Hovel,
I strip to bra and boxers.
A fierce tug at a postcard
and several fly out.

The one between my thumb and forefinger
works well for this moment.

"Mosaic—The Drunken Dionysus—
4th Cent. A.D.—Found in Antioch"

Intricate placement of tiny tiles
depicting the god of grape juice
leaning heavily
on some youth,
his wine cup spilling
into a groveling cur's mouth below.

DEAREST CAROLE,

REMEMBER WHEN AMY CAME HOME AT 3 A.M. VOMITING FUMES OF TEQUILA? REMEMBER I TRIED TO HELP HER? WITH A COLD WET CLOTH ON THE BACK OF HER NECK? AND YOU CAME IN AND TOOK THE CLOTH FROM ME SAYING "I'LL TAKE CARE OF IT." LIKE I COULDN'T DO IT MYSELF.

AND I SAID TO YOU AGAIN WE NEED TO DO SOMETHING ABOUT THIS. AND YOU IGNORED ME.

REMEMBER THAT?

AND THEN AMY WENT TO THE BEACH PARTY THREE NIGHTS LATER AND

DIDN'T COME HOME.

REMEMBER THAT?

SO MUCH LOVE,

VERA

I need company to stop my brain.
After lumpy mashed potato dinner
I don Tevas and open my door
to find Milo
crossing over from the Merc.

I walk heavily partway up the drive
to meet him.

He takes my shoulders
with his restful strong hands,
saying
"I was coming to tell you,
MaryBeth called.
The boy is holding on
but he probably won't walk
and he hasn't awoken yet."

Milo's deep voice breaks,
and I am concentrating
on the glittery gray stubbles
at the base of his cleft chin,

the level of my eyes.

Not many people have
cleft chins, I think,
then shake myself a bit.

"Um, good," I say,
feeling inadequate,
but the inside of my head
feels empty and hazy-bright.

Milo tilts his head down a bit
so he is looking at me
    through his eyebrows,
dragging my eyes to his.
"How are you doing?" he says.

"He'll probably die," I state,
thinking it's a funny place to discuss death
right in the middle of a dirt driveway.
Or maybe it's the perfect place

to discuss death.

Milo's eyes have widened a little.

"We don't know that," he says
comfortingly.

But I don't need comforting.
"It looked bad, Milo,"
I say matter-of-factly
"I don't think he'll make it.
These things happen."

The low sun is crisping my right shoulder.

I feel him gazing at me.

In my head I can see
the dusty devastated father
emerging from the mine,
and then

the wet hair clinging
to the boy's blanched forehead.

A tear burbles over.

Milo touches my arm.
"Vera—" he starts.

"A few weeks ago
my little sister Amy disappeared,
in the ocean,
she was swimming,"
I tumble words.
"Oh, Milo, she is the same age,"
and I sob into the shelter
of my sunburned elbow.

Milo gathers me in his arms.

I calm slowly,
his belly warmer
than the sun setting on my back.

Cooler this morning.
As I come off the trail
and onto gravel,
I hear the raised voices of
Andrew and Hoben in the trailer
and stop where I am.

"I can't believe you are thinking it's Dakota!
Have you even talked with him?"
Hoben's high, fierce voice
matches his small, wiry frame.
"Why the hell not?
He's the one you should—"

Hoben is the tinderbox of the group,
and I hear Lon
patting his feathers down
in a calming hush.

"It's *bullshit*, man," Hoben spits.
"None of us took it.
And we don't know anything."

Now Andrew says in angry calm,
"You have us all here
because you trust us.
So trust us,"
and suddenly he and Hoben
come clattering down the Airstream steps
and I throw myself into
what I hope is casual forward motion
onto the noisy
crushed
schist.

"Hi, guys!" I chirp,
sounding like a fucking
cheerleader.

Apprehension going in,
but once I'm inside
Lon just grunts,
"Good. You are here.
Got a ton of work for you."

He glances up,
flicks the requisite switch,
and for two one-thousandths of a second
his lips cramp up
like they want to form
a stylish smile
but it
so
does not get there.

Scooping up the turds of his work,
he paces out
into daylight.

Paperback-entrenched,
but the unusual sound of
inebriated rock hounds singing on Main
pulls me out,
and I listen till they fade again.

I find I am resting eyes on the postcard drawer,
so I propeller my legs out of bed
and stand cold-footed,
toes of the left foot on top of the right.

A quick thought of Lon
and his shifting sands
aggravates me,
and my hand picks out a very old postcard.

"Bears at Yellowstone" in that quaint
  twig-looking font.

Wow, is this inappropriate,
a photo of people feeding their lunch
out the station wagon window

directly into the well-toothed mouth of

a mama bear with her two cubs.

I'd be terrified that close,

sturdy 1960s car

or no car.

Don't feed the bears.

The arid wind builds
and I will let
Tilly cook me something for dinner.

The menu says
    STEAK TIPS
in fancy writing
and I decide to believe
it might be like
beef Stroganoff.

I do not dare watch Tilly
prepare this dish
because I don't really want to know,
so I twirl my red stool
around to watch
small objects fly by
in the wildness out the window.

A dish is plunked heavily at my place
and I turn back
to see

a large steamy pile of
brown-on-brown-on-brown.

I think it's steak on gravy on noodles
but it tastes like rock salt.

Before I take a second bite,
Tilly wipes a finger along the plate rim
removing a few drips.

She licks her finger and shrugs.
"Real chefth do that," she says proudly.

Good thing I am
really
hungry.

In the still of morning
I am awakened by dull cramps,
making me wonder about
my brown dinner.

As they get sharper,
I remember where I stashed
tampons,
and tramp
outside to the outhouse.

There is debris
everywhere after last night's windstorm.

And when I come back toward
the garden,
I shriek.

The seedlings are toast,
shriveled black and lying flat
in the parched soil.

"No, no!" I whisper,
bending to touch them.

I swear as another cramp comes
and stalk in
for some ibuprofen.

“It dried them out,” whispers Pearl,
ringlets shining in sunlight.
“This climate is very challenging for seedlings.”

She is still nodding pleasantly,
gazing upward at a circling vulture.
“Yes, well, and you could have started the seeds
in little pots indoors first, you know,
let them get larger and stronger,
and then planted them out,
you could have done that, yes.”

What?

“You didn’t *tell* me that!
Why didn’t you *tell* me that
when I started?
You just let me kill those plants?
Maybe a little communication would help here!”

I heft my white-hot anger
and trudge away
from her unnaturally vibrant Eden.

Kicking viciously
at small rocks
I send dust clouds
roiling behind as I climb the path
toward the mine entrance.

"Fucking Pearly-Whirl," I spit.
Here I am asking for help
and she only tells me half the story.

The outsider again.
Out of place,
with no one letting me in.

Not Rob and Tanya.
    I kick out at a hunk of quartz.
Not Lon
and his damn
Secondary Packaging secrets.
    Kick another rock.
Not 'Roley
and her fucking

I'll-take-care-of-it-you-just-stand-aside
control crap.

Hard kick at the mine's metal entrance
supports,
and I lunge with gravity,
grabbing rust with my hand
to keep from falling.

I face the mine's dark maw,
realizing I stand where
the unconscious boy was carried out,
and start to cry,
brain disconnected from
ragged metal biting my fingers.

Then comes her familiar giggle,
and I whip to my left
to see
less than fifteen feet away,
Amy.

"Amy?" I whisper,
but it's her,
it's her,
laughing and twirling away
in that irritating
taunt
she's done since she was two,
but now I love it
I love it
I love her
and—

"Amy!" I call out,
but she's bounding off boulders,
zigging away,
dark hair
pennanting behind
in the wind she creates.

"AMY!" I yell,
scrambling to a stand.

She is almost a speck now,
running west.

It's really her.

And suddenly
that terrifies me.

I limp up the Hovel steps,
stop
and limp back down,
mindlessly recognizing
a need to pee.

I am not nuts, right?

It was Amy.

I make it as far as the supposed garden
and sink down next to the
parching earth.

Digging with a finger
I find
soil so dead I am crying again.

To my left,

one more seedling
  having pushed through
now withers to sleep,
bleached of chlorophyll,
returning to dust.

She talked to me.
Impossible.
But
it was Amy.

Holed up in the Hovel
with locked doors
paperbacks
potatoes
and
a powerful need to pupate.

Twenty-four hours.

I have work to do for Milo
and yes,
even Lon,
but first,
twenty-four hours.

The postcard I pull
says only
"St. Roch"
with a black-and-white photo of a brigantine
locked in ice.

The tide is out.

Foot-thick ice holds the ship high,
stern up,
keel showing,
total displacement.

DEAR CAROLE,

I AM SCARED. AMY IS DEAD. ISN'T SHE?
I KEEP SEEING HER.
SOMETHING IS NOT RIGHT.

I can't even sign the postcard.
I stash it
in the file folder
like an innocent.

“Hey-ro, Vera,” Milo calls from his wheel.

He is head-down,
ponytail dusting the floor,
examining the bottom edge of a newly thrown
pot.

“How’d you know it was me?” I ask.

His upside-down grin
looks a bit menacing.

“Who else visits me?” he answers,
veins in his forehead bulging.
“And it’s the desert.
Can’t sneak up on anyone
in this quiet and crunch.”

He scuffs the gravel
with a sandal.

As I take experimental steps,

listening to the sharp voice of edged stone,
it occurs to me.

Did I hear any noise
when Amy ran?

I can't remember.

I rub a hand over my face.
Maybe I need a vacation from this place.

I feel my mouth drop
and the heat of the Airstream enters,
warming my tongue.

"You want me to what?"

Lon is writing checks
at the trailer desk
not looking up.
"Itsa long way, and I can't spare the guys.
You're gonna have to take this package to Blake
in Destin."

Thrill lights up nerves,
a physical zing to the last three fingers
of my left hand.

"Am I walking?" I say brightly.

"Take the Duster.
Tomorrow morning.
Keys," he grunts, pointing to the hook.

“’Kay,” I say, breathless.
“Thanks, Lon!”

“Yuh,” he says,
but he doesn’t even glance at me
to catch my grin.

I bounce out the screen door,
sprint to the Hovel,
and clomp back to the bedroom
to retrieve my maps.

Road trip!

Up at four a.m.
wearing my headlamp to guide me
    to the trailer
finding directions with the package
collecting Lon's car keys
placing the note on peeling Formica

GONE ON DELIVERY
—VERA

and out the perforated door.

Once I'm at the Duster,
I move in high gear—
door open
jump in
find the ignition with my index finger
key in
turn
clutch
fuel
blast outta here!

Spraying dirt in a giant rooster tail
I'm on the road,
pounding heart
pounding the dash
crowing loud!

No one is up here
on the mountain.

I'm too early
to meet the guy in Destin yet,
and this historical site is marked on my map.

When the dust from Lon's Plymouth settles
I am entranced by the view
in my side mirror
and forget to actually get out of the car.

Charcoal kilns.
Immense stone beehives
line the edge of the road,
like altars to human ingenuity and geology
here in the piñon pine forest at high elevation.

Tough to smelt the ore for silver
in a place like Death Valley
where wood fuel is pretty much
nowhere to be seen.

These were the only trees for the miners to cut
for miles.

I roll my window down
still looking in the mirror,
knives of dry sharp altitude
slicing my nostrils.

Absolutely silent at 6:17 a.m.

Swinging from the car
I glance into the backseat at the package
and decide to reroll the window
and lock the door.

I'm sure this is illegal,
climbing the back of the charcoal kiln
to the smoke window
fifteen feet off the ground,
but I've done a bunch of rock climbing
and I can't resist.

Who would arrest me?
A helluva drive up Wildrose Canyon,
not a ranger to be seen.

Rocks are mortared in
sticking out every which way.
Simple to find handholds
but hot in the blistering sun
and sharp.

I reach the window,
turning to scootch
onto the ledge,
my head knocking the arch of bricks.

I gaze uphill to the peak,
the wind wooing the piñon pines,
echo-chuckling around ridges,
and I realize
I have not seen real trees
for what seems like
a long time.
Makes me miss last summer's geo trip
in Mammoth.
Real trees and laughter.

The breeze drops.
Silence.

Damn, it's hot in Death Valley in August.

At least my ass
inside the kiln window in the dark
is cooling off.

Frickin' tape.
The package on the passenger seat keeps
  popping open
like a devious Xmas present.
Usually there is a strap around Lon's packages,
but this box is really small.

When I firm the flap down
the tape comes off in my fingers
and the package drops to the floor of the car.

Shit!

Don't drop it, you idiot!
Artifacts are fragile!

I pick it up and shake it gingerly,
listening for the *kichink*
of broken something—

nothing.
Whew.

But the untaped end is blasted open
  from the fall.

I can just see printing on the box.
Ease it open just a little more—

Albers Corn Meal?

I shake the box again
a little harder.
Nothing shifts inside.
A little peek under the first layer of pack—

I have the sudden childish thought that
I'm the good girl.
I don't want to know what's in the box.

Refold the flap.
I press the used tape firmly.
A length of mint dental floss from the Duster's
  glove compartment
ties it neatly.

Destin's a seedy little three-building town.
Heart bumping a bit
I ask at the counter
for the guy I'm delivering to, Blake.
Heart jumping up
past code yellow
when they come out
to tell me to go in the back room.

Blake's a huge round meatloaf of a man,
unsmiling
sweating in a black tee.
He just holds out his hand
for the package
and with a breeze of onions
leaves through a side door to check it out.
Quickly back,
flashing a gold molar,
holding out a ringed hand to shake.

I'm climbing into the Duster,
my hand still aching from Blake's grip.

I grin in tension,
drive nicely out of the lot,
and grin wider as I hit the road
45 mph in second gear.

For the amount of money, hell,
that was
easy.

"Hey," Lon says curtly
from the table
as I open the trailer door.
"Have a fun trip?"

He is not using a
friendly tone.
He erases something vigorously
without looking up.

I sidle over cautiously.

Brushing away the erasings,
he states,
"Not much work today.
Take a hike or something."

I stand still,
confused,
buffeted by the gusts
of his obvious anger.

When he continues his work
without saying more,
I turn on the ball of my foot
and leave,
only realizing when I am outside
that I didn't
say
one
word.

Bouncing on my bedsprings,
turning on my phone
against better judgment.

Two more phone calls
one from Carole,
one from—

Amy?

Apparently I have teleported
to the backyard
and past the dying garden
and through the outhouse door
and I am screaming something
and my cell phone is flying out of my hand
and down into the dank
  and slightly stenchy dark
of the one-holer.

I think I threw it on purpose.

Except,
the phone is on, right?

Imagine peeing at midnight
and having it ring.

Hell no.

So now I am gently prying off
the shit box boards with a hammer
    from the shack,
sliding in the side
with stomach tight
to keep my body
close to the edge,
away from the
nasty
    but hey, not too nasty
dung heap in the middle.

Takes a second to find my phone
because I did not

remember my frickin' headlamp.
It landed in a clean corner—
    the desert miracle.

I make myself replace the boards
before calling in for the message.

Heart is pounding,
brain is faint.
The hammer I hold
seems to glow golden
around its edges.

Then a soft voice,
"Vera? I was hoping you'd answer
if I used Amy's phone
to call. . . ."
Carole is crying.

I press delete.

Small-town barbecue this afternoon
in back of the Merc,
and I feel silly
but kind of excited to put on
clean(er) pants
and an actual buttoned shirt,
    except it's wrinkled like desiccated fruit
so
clean(er) pants
and an actual unstained T-shirt.
Oh heck,
different earrings than the silver I've
worn every day.
The gray pearl ones that Carole gave me.

There is no one in this town of Garrett
  under forty.
I'm not going to impress
the *permanentes*,
and I know Lon and the boys were
not invited.

Still.

The Moth would say
"It's nice to feel one's best."

Gag.

Still.

I even scrubbed my Tevas.

At the barbecue
almost everyone is paired off with a beer.
Or three or four.

I am the only person without one.
I am standing by the food.
Such as it is.

Oh. Except Milo, over there.
He's drinking root beer,
like me.

"No, not Milo," Tilly told me.
"No alcohol for him."

She shakes her head solemnly
and waits for me to ask.

"Hith partner in Needlth
wath killed by a drunk driver.
Drove right up on the thidewalk

and flattened poor Jacob againtht the concrete
wall of the courthouthe."

I gape at her.

She shrugs and starts to walk away.
"People get thtupid, kill thomeone."

Huh.

"People get stupid and kill themselves, too,"
I say to the bowl of Little Smokies sausages.

The Hovel smells different when I walk in.

I tread softly,
feeling forearm hair rise.

I do not say
"Hello?" like idiots do in movies
but I also don't take time
to remove my shoes.

Through the living room
into the bedroom,
breathlessly easing the bathroom door.

No one.

But the floorboards in the bathroom
are squicked up
a centimeter.

I would never leave them like that.

My heart takes a rest
from beating three seconds
and the contraction that comes
is a doozy.

Everything out from under the boards,
I scrabble my fingers around
in the dark corners,
making sure it's really gone.

No one new in town today.
None of the locals would take my money.

One of the boys?
Lon?

They don't seem to need money.
But there has been a shitload of anger
running around there.

Who else would it be?

I blow into the floor space
ejecting at least
seventy years of sub-footing dust
into my eyes.

Squinting,
crying,
angry about my $500.

I have to go see Lon.

When I get to the trailer
Lon is doing paperwork.

With five $100 bills sitting there whistling dixie
on the table.

I breathe.

"Is that my money?"
My voice quakes a little and I fight it.

"Wha?" Lon says, not looking up.

"Is that my money?"

"Well," he says,
turning in a smooth rolling movement
to tilt his dark head at me,
"I thought I would hold it
for the time being.
Until I find out what's going on

with you."

I feel a little spinny
and grasp the counter
of the stupid tiny kitchenette.

"What's going *on* with me?" I repeat,
feeling slow.
Is he going to ask about Amy?

Lon is looking almost pleasant,
but in the way that
a cobra might look pleasant.
"Let me ask you a question," he says,
his edges appearing glittery to me.

"Fine. Go ahead!" I say,
shrugging,
heart hammering.

"*Why*, Vera,

did you open the package
before delivering it to Blake?"
Lon is looking decidedly less pleasant now.

"Open it? No.
I *closed* it.
The paper had popped open and I—"

"You tied it up with dental floss,
most ingenious, yes.
But why did you open the package in the first
place?"
Lon is still glittery
and venomous,
and I am really confused.

"I—I didn't!" There is a high pitch
to my voice
that makes me feel like
it might not actually be mine.
Maybe the Moth's.

I take a deep breath.
"Why *would* I open it?" I say,
starting to get angry.
"It's just pottery and art and stuff, right?
What's the big secret?"
I actually stamp the floor,
something I will feel idiotic for later
but I am pissed and scared.

Lon is still as a serpent,
eyes black.
"What is in the boxes
is none of your business,"
he says quietly.

"Fine!" I shout.
"I didn't *look* in the fucking *box*!
Give me back my *money*!"

He sits another minute
before sweeping the bills off the table

and holding them out to me.
"I believe you," he says graciously,
as if he is doing me a favor.

"Oh, *thank* you, my liege," I say sarcastically,
grabbing my money
and swinging out the screen door.

I pound over the ridge to Milo's.

He is bent over in the shade
scraping out a glaze bucket,
and looks up at my hard footsteps.

"Hey, Veer," he says carefully,
watching my face.

I hold out my $100 bills.
"Do you have somewhere you can
keep these for me?
Somewhere *safe*?"
My tone is harsh,
so I add a softer
"Please?" after a beat.

Milo's bushy eyebrows have risen.
He slowly puts the bucket down,
wiping his hands

on clay-covered pants,
and places his palm on my shoulder.

"Come inside the house," he says gently.

Milo's kitchen is cool
and in my anger I only notice
spots of turquoise around me
    instead of objects.

Milo pours me some lemonade.
I take a gulp
and the sour swoosh
rearranges my focus.

Now I notice that his fridge is turquoise
    and his round-faced clock
    and a metal cookie jar shaped like the
        pyramids at Giza.

He pats a wooden stool,
but I stay standing.

He waits till I drain my glass.

Then he raises those wiry eyebrows at me
expectantly.

Milo doesn't interrupt me once.

When I am done
his face looks dark,
thunderous.

"So am I understanding that
  Lon stole your money?
Is that correct?"

I take a step back,
considering.
"Well, he took it, but he gave it back."

Milo shakes his head.
"He broke into your house—"

"It isn't locked!" I say,
laughing a little.

Milo stops,
gazing at me sternly.

"He went into your house
without permission.
He went into your bathroom
and pried up the floorboards
without permission.
He took your money
and left with it."
Milo hasn't stopped looking into my eyes.
"Is that correct?" he adds softly.

I nod,
swallowing.

Well, when you put it like that . . .

My money in Milo's safe,
I walk wearily back to the Hovel.

Looking forward to taking off my boots
and a good dose
of mashed potatoes.

Maybe I'll even soak my feet
in mashed potatoes.

This is such a delicious thought
that I get almost to the steps of the Hovel
before I notice Lon is sitting on them,
chin in his hand.

I stop abruptly,
right hand on my hip.

Lon holds his hand up,
and if it were another less angry moment
I would laugh at its similarity
to the old

How!

Indian greeting in the Westerns.

But Lon looks sad,

and I wait.

"I came to say I am sorry," he says,

eyes brown and soft.

I snort.

I am stirring bubbling potatoes,
poking around with a fork.

"So if someone is stealing art from you,"
I say finally,
still controlling my temper,
"why would you assume it's me?
You've barely told me a
thing about the business!"

Lon is standing in the living room
almost imperceptibly
rocking from foot to foot,
his brow creased.

"I know, I know," he says,
running his hand through slick hair.
"But I can't believe it's
one of my guys.
We're like *brothers*."

I clang the fork

with unnecessary force
against the pot's edge.
"Well at least *one* of them isn't acting
like your brother."

"Hoben backed you," Lon goes on.
"Said you were too clean-girl to steal.
Andrew seemed unsure of everyone.
But *someone* is taking items, that I know."

"It's not me," I state firmly,
draining the pot.
Clean-girl, huh?
Picking up my prized masher,
I pause over the potatoes.

"Would you like some mashed?"
I ask
a little coldly,
but at least polite.

The Moth would be so proud.

"No, uh, I should go."
He turns back at the door.
"I hope you'll work day after tomorrow?" he asks
then mutters to himself,
"Gotta keep things going."

I flatten potatoes through the steam
for a moment,
letting him wait.

"Yuh," I grunt at him.

I am overstuffed
with potatoes and betrayal
and don't fucking feel like
washing dishes.

Postcard.

"Pacific Northwest Wagner Festival—*Die Walküre*—Act I"

Ha! How appropriate.
Tanya and I went with her parents
to this opera.

So Act I of *The Valkyrie*
has Siegmund showing up at
Sieglinde's house
asking for shelter
because he killed someone
related to Sieglinde's husband Hunding
trying to save some bride from
a forced marriage,

and Siegmund stays the night
    if you know what I mean
and there's a big fight
and Sieglinde drugs her husband and sings a lot.

This confusion is kind of how I felt
after Carole blew off my fears for Amy,
and I went to gripe
to my two best friends
only to find
Rob and Tanya in full-tongue kiss mode,
and then they tell me
not only are they
in love,
they're going
to Spain
without me.

The whole opera is five frickin' hours.

I am pretty sure

I don't have the
patience
to sit through
an opera
ever
again.

In the morning
I tie down a bandanna
against the wind's argumentative tone,
trying to keep my hair clean-ish
one more day.

It's a relief to wear my Tevas
instead of boots
and I scuff up to Milo's
to help package up pottery.

Holding my breath
against a peppering wind,
I remember something Lon said.

Just like the Hopi pots from Lon,
Milo's beautiful cups and plates
get sent away
to people in places far from this desert.

But the people buying Milo's coffee cups
get friendly e-mails and phone calls.

They hear his raucous laugh,
his thoughts on what makes a handle comfy,
and sometimes
they get his personal recipe for barbecue sauce.

That is a connection.
Pottery as a connection to a person,
the man who lovingly created
what they bought.

The handwritten note from Milo
tacked to the door
says he's on an errand.

So I let myself in
and package up the pots
he's left for me,
which doesn't take even till ten a.m.

The wind has died a bit
as I leave,
and I decide I could use
a good rock hunt for a few hours.

I stop by the Hovel
for my boots,
and head west
with a rock hammer
and my water pack,
happy in the solitary freedom
of glinting desert brilliance.

"Beauteous-beauteous-beauteous!"
I am singing,
jigging across my little living room,
holding the chunk of quartz
reverently over my head.

I bring it down to eye level
eyeing the sweet crinkle of honest gold
nestled in the rock's crack.

And then I notice.

My bedroom door is
just about closed.

I always prop it open with a brick.
Always.

Clutching my quartz,
I tap the bedroom door
and it swings.

Hold my breath,
one step in,
look to the left.

The floorboards in the bathroom
are up again,
my folder splayed open on the floor,
empty.

I remember hiding my quartz
in the shrubs next door.

I remember dumping water
from my jug
over my head
as I set out.

I do not remember
anything else
till I am in the Airstream
standing over Lon
yelling
"What the fuck is going on?"

Lon has something twitching in his lip.
On the table are
four postcards
fanned in a decorative display.

I breathe,
and my veins fill with metallic blood.

"Apparently you have something of mine,"
I say more calmly.

The twitch in Lon's lip moves upward
into an unpleasant smirk.

"And you had something of mine,"
he says quietly.

What?
"I don't have anything of yours."

Lon reaches behind him,
drawing out
an intricately patterned Native American bowl
wrapped loosely in packing paper.
"You don't have it *anymore*," he states.
"I retrieved it from under your porch
where you hid it."

I stare at it.
"That?" I exclaim.

"What the fuck are you talking about?"

Lon leans back,
hands in back of his head,
biceps flexing
to impress somebody.

"You deny it?" he said.

"You better believe I deny it!
Listen, Lon,
you already accused me of stealing from you
and then you apologized and everything
and I forgave you
and came back to work.
What is *wrong* with you?"

He leans forward,
crow's-feet next to his narrowed eyes
grasping the edge of his face.

"What is wrong with me?"

Lon's voice is edgy and high.
"I trusted you!
I trusted you!
I took you in and gave you a job,
trusted you with my business books,
gave you some purpose
    while you run away from home!
I trusted you like family!"
Lon's teeth are showing as
his breath grates in and out.

I place my palms on the table,
looking into his eyes.
"You took me *in*?
What am I,
a pet?
Gave me purpose with your rocket-surgery job
of adding two-digit numbers?
And I did *not* run away from home!"

After a few seconds eye to eye,
Lon relaxes back on the vinyl,

caressing a postcard edge with his fingertip.
"It seems there might be, ah,
sensitive info in these missives.
Things you wouldn't want known,
perhaps."
I draw in a short breath,
sharp as the glint from gravel
outside the trailer.

"They are personal to *me*.
No one else cares," I say through my teeth.

Lon turns toward his business,
tapping his stack of invoices
into a neat pile.
"I think of the postcards as collateral.
I will keep them until I know
for certain
why my art was at your house."

I throw my hands up in the air.
"You are nuts, Lon.

I did not steal anything from you.
Go ahead and keep the postcards."

I turn to leave.

"Seen your dead sister Amy lately?" he says
softly.

My vision goes white a moment,
slick and soft
as marshmallow,
and then I stride out of the trailer
through radiant gravel.

I am stomping over the first ridge.

Fuck. What will Lon do?
And hell, maybe I don't care if he
tells the world I'm nuts,
seeing a dead sister and shit.
Who would he tell?
He doesn't have access to anyone—

Wait.
I put Carole's address on that card.
That one card. Shit.
Shit shit.

I clock a rock with my heel and go down hard,
knees and palms in the edgy stones.
I'm enjoying the pain
and start sobbing on all fours,
feeling disconnected again,
gathering the pain in my palm,

loving the pain.

And someone is there.

I look up, shading my wincing eyes to see a
backlit figure.
“Ouch,” Amy says, gesturing.
“You really took a dive, V.”

My heart stops.

Blood trickles down
my raised forearm.

And as my heart starts up again,
I feel that runaway adrenaline.
I launch myself to standing,
grabbing for Amy's long hair,
screaming rage as it streams by.
She dances away,
sparkling laughter,
and I race after her.
She spins in circles,
dodging gracefully as I lunge to grab her,
wordless swears pouring from my mouth.
I feel so weighted,
heavy and clumsy,
and my lungs are shredding with desert heat,
my throat choking,
and finally I double over and bellow,

"Go away, you dead fucking bitch! Go away and leave me alone! Go!"

Bloody hands stuck to the skin of my knees,
I sob,
snot running over my gaping mouth
as I grab breath.
"I don't care if I'm crazy,
just leave me *alone*!"

I collapse crying and squeeze my eyes shut,
lying down on the dirt,
one hand still glued to my leg
  with oozing blood,
wailing,
drooling,
my cheek pressing into tiny sharp rocks.

My small bathroom
is comforting.
I rinse my face,
gingerly douse my palm,
dab caked blood off my knee
with a wet T-shirt.

Leaning on the cold sink
in just my underwear,
I sigh.

I've kind of had it with myself.

I wait for Wind Dog to buy his salami
and leave
before I go up to pay.

Potatoes and vodka.

First I thought I'd get a mixer
to go with it,
but I don't like tomato juice
with or without alcohol,
and orange juice from concentrate is nasty.

Tilly doesn't say anything.
I feel itchy as I wait for change,
wondering why she doesn't card me.

I lay the bottle at the bottom
of my green nylon sack,
but I don't like the way
the shape
is so
obvious.

So I shift the potatoes
to be on the bottom,
then the Smirnoff.

Fussing way too long.

I'm outta here.

In the Hovel
I put the potatoes away
and sit and watch the vodka bottle
as it stands firmly
motionless on the counter.

I will never know
unless I try it,
right?

I crack open the top,
wafting the fumes toward my nose
like we learned in chemistry.

"Never lean in and take a deep breath!"
Mrs. Gantz used to say.
"Waft! Waft!
Keep your nose clean and healthy!"

Vodka does not smell like much.

I mean
it reeks of alcohol
but it's like there's no other scent.

I pour an inch into a glass.

"Here goes!"
I take a swig,
gasp through the fire
and cough half of it into my hair.

Hair tied back,
breath moving through lungs cleanly,
I try again.

Maybe water.
Don't people drink vodka
and tonic water?

I pour half water
half alcohol,
and this batch goes down
more smoothly.

There seems to be exhaust
coming out of my windpipe
and that warm feeling
is reaching my gut.

I think I'll sit down.

I don't know howlong

itsbeen

buttheresaknockon thedoor.

I think I'm holleringcomein

and

suddenlyMiloshere

graspingmywrist

alittlehard

andaskingifI'mokayI'mokayI'mokayI'mgonnabe
sick—

"I don't want any more water!"
I am sullen,
but not as queasy.

"Too bad, Vera!" Milo says cheerfully,
handing me the cup.

"Mgonna drown," I grump,
but I drink it
because he's been here
    tolerating me awhile
and he's pretty much cured me
just with kindness and H_2O.
And cleaned up after me.

Milo plunks down on the chair
and thumps his fist gently
three times
on the counter.

"So. What's all this about?
Vodka does not seem your thing."

I finish my water
and scrub my fingers through my curls.

"Well, now I know."
I grin a little sheepishly,
    my mouth feeling lopsided.
"Amy drank a lot at the end,
she partied with her friends,
and I am pissed at her for it,
but what do *I* know?
I never drink."
I pick up the cup again,
drain the last three drops,
and set it back down.
"I *never* drink.
The Moth is always sipping something
and she's not"—
    I take a deep breath—
"not the person I want to be.

"So I'm out in the desert. . . ."
I gesture widely and

Milo stabilizes the empty water glass.
"In this big desert,
isn't this a good place for alcohol?
No one around to get hurt."

Milo smiles slightly.
"Except perhaps you," he says.

"Well, at least I wasn't going to
kill myself with it,"
I say irritably.

Milo looks sad.

"And then haunt people," I add.

Oops. I wasn't going to talk about this.

Milo says "Haunt people?" in a curious way.

I laugh a little.
I mean,
it's going to sound so stupid
that I see my dead sister
and I don't know if it's a ghost
or a hallucination
and honestly,
neither
one
is
okay
with
me.

I'm finishing crying
and Milo has a comforting arm
over my shoulder
and he finally
says something.

"Death is a hard thing, Veer.
The brain in denial is a powerful tool.
I think perhaps you haven't
finished dealing with Amy's death."

Sounds pretty logical
but I don't feel logical about it.

"You think I'm nuts?" I ask.

"Nope," says Milo.
"Maybe seeing her
these couple of times
is a way to finally say
good-bye."

"Say good-bye?
More like she's torturing me.
Like little sisters *always* do."

Milo is nodding.
"Exactly," he says.

We sit.

"Did you see hallucinations of Jacob
after he died?" I ask,
afraid of the answer.

Milo is quiet
and then he sniffs.
"No," he says softly.

He wipes a drip from his nose.
"Well, maybe.
I used to think I saw Jacob
out of the corner of my eye,

glimpses,
you know?
At the grocery store,
one aisle over, or
walking up the driveway.
I think I needed a change of place
to stop the reminders,
to help recover."
He sighs.

"But you"
    he laughs a little
"*you* needed a change of place
and took the pain *with* you."

"Huh," I say,
laughing too.

I pull on a lock of my loose hair.

"I feel like I don't have
solid rock under me.

There *or* here."
My voice trembles.

"Ah, Veer."
He squeezes me
and rests his head briefly
against mine.
"Where was the last place
you felt that
solid rock?"

"Last summer's geo dig
at Devils Postpile,
with Wendy and Peg."

I surprise myself
with how quickly
that answer comes.

My morning shower leaves me
still feeling parched.
The sun is blasting
like the fusion furnace it is,
and at six thirty a.m. it's dry enough to
mummify my tea bag
from last night.

There is a knock on the front door.

As I hesitate,
in the quiet
I hear the soft whop
of chopper blades
in the distance.

I finally walk through the living room,
flipping my hair to dry it,
and open the door
to find Tilly.

"Go on up to Milo'th," she commands.

"Dempthey went by earlier,
and there'th been trouble."

I automatically slide into my Tevas,
stepping out into the heat.

"What kind of trouble, Tilly?"

She has grasped my upper arm,
pointing me uphill.

"Yethterday Milo talked to Lon
about thome money Lon took from you?
And now the pottery shed is in shamblth.
Go!"
and she pushes my shock-worn habitus
toward Milo's.

“It’s just mud, Vera.”
Milo is sweeping curving crescents of
greenware,
small dusty bits and
large scoops still capacious enough to hold soup.

“Just *mud*?
You had made it something else, Milo!”
It takes me a stark moment
of crimson anger
to realize
I am not even helping him.
I forcefully grab a short-bristled broom,
knocking over a rake with a clatter.

“It is just mud,
and you learn that as a potter,”
he says lightly with a slight smile
as he sweeps.
“I break my pots all the time.”

“*You* didn’t break these, Milo, *they* did!

Did they come fuck up your life
last night
while you were helping me
not fuck up mine?"
Sweeping with too much muscle,
I send a broken mug
sailing
against the wooden door.

"I don't know when this happened.
But I didn't see it till this morning."
Milo stops his work and looks at me.
"It is just mud,
and I will make more pots."

"We can report them, you know—"

"Report whom?"
Milo has not changed position.
"We don't have any proof of who it was."

I snort. "We know who it—"

"No," he states,
re-administering his broom.
"We don't know."

"Well, *I* know—"

"Vera—"

"*I* will report them, then!"

"No!" Milo raises his voice slightly.
"With no proof,
it is not worth that exercise."

"But—"

In staccato meter,
he says "It is just mud,"
as angry as I've seen him.
With me?

Tears flood my eyes and I glare at him.
"So you do nothing?
Give up?"

Milo picks up the base of a teapot
and crumbles it in his heavy hands.
For a moment I think he's not going to say
anything else.
Then he takes a short breath.
"I have learned when to accept.
When that is the best response."

"But—"

"For *me*, Vera," he says gently,
dusting his fingers.
"The best response for me.
Is to accept pain and move forward."

I throw the stubby broom down and

stomp out
past the turquoise glaze poured in the dirt,
spelling out

LEAVE NOW GAY-BOY

I am twenty steps down-trail
sniffing hard
wiping tears,
when I hear a gunshot
far off to the right of me.

And then another,
sharp and pinging,
a ricochet.

"Vera?" Milo's voice comes from behind me
shrill and scared.

"I'm here!" I yell,
and hear his truck start up.

In a few moments he's pulled beside me
leaning to throw the passenger door open.

"Get in!" he commands.

"Sounds like Lon's place," I say,

scrambling with my seat belt
as we bounce over boulders.

"Yep," says Milo,
grim.

I am shocked to see a shotgun in his lap.

"Everyone's got one in the desert, Veer," he says
without humor.

Except me.
Yikes.

When three sheriff's cars roar up the road
Milo pulls onto the ridge
letting them pass.

We idle with the windows down,
listening.

"Give them a chance to deal with it,"
murmurs Milo.
Sweat dribbles down to his jaw.

The AC freezes spots on my arm and stomach,
the fryolator window edge sizzling my
underarm.

Inside I have ice-cream headache,
my swirling thoughts a few minutes ago
chilled
crystallizing
mid-chaos.

I think nothing.

A heat fly settles on my arm
hoping for a salt lick.

"Hear that?" Milo says,
turning his head toward town.

More sirens,
gaining volume,
and soon an ambulance
and two more sheriffs bound past,
spraying rocks,
raising dust.

Sand settles.

We sit.

I shift my right arm inside the truck
aiming my elbow for a blast of AC.

I can't decide if I am worried for Lon.
Or any of the other guys.

And it could be an accidental thing,
right?

You hear about people cleaning a gun,
having it go off.
Happens all the time.

My elbow is cold
and I put it on the window again.

Outside the idling truck,
the desert is so quiet.

Milo sighs,
deep and rumbling.

I roll a soft bitterness
over my tongue.
"I didn't *ask* you to go
talk to Lon about my money
and get your pottery all broken," I say.
"I already had the money back."

"I know, I'm sorry." Milo sighs again.
"I was upset for you,
but it wasn't my place to take care of it."

I rub my sun-roasted elbow.
Adults don't apologize often.
Maybe none of us does.
"I'm sorry I got mad
you didn't want to tell the police," I say.

Milo's right hand reaches over
and gently smothers my left
on the seat between us
for just a second.

"Learning another person's ways is hard,
Veer.
We're learning each other,
that's all."
He smiles,
transforming back into
the relaxed happy man
I suddenly feel
may be my only friend.

After sitting a bit longer,
I notice Milo beginning to
jig his leg up and down.

"How long do we wait?" I ask,
knowing I sound impatient
but feeling like I've *been*
pretty damn
patient.

Milo laughs a little,
shoving the gear stick home
to start the engine.
"Probably long enough
for both of us," he says
as we pull back onto the dirt road.

We bounce onward
finally coming over the ridge
to see a mass of activity
at Secondary Packaging,
trucks
police
EMTs
and
a ranger's green vehicle.

My heart is pumping hard,
but
sheriffs are moving calmly.
EMTs lean on their rig.

"Must not be too serious,"
Milo mutters.

A sheriff comes toward us,
holding his hand up,
and Milo cranes out his window.

"Everything okay, Jank?" Milo asks.

"You *know* him?" I whisper.

Jank nods, relaxed,
though he doesn't smile.
"No one hurt, Milo.
Quite the scuffle, though.
I think we're settling out."
He peers down inside the truck.

"I'd put that away.
No need to excite anyone."

Milo stuffs his gun under the bench seat.

"You hear gunshots,
you never know, Jank," he says.

The sheriff nods again,
patting the roof of the truck,
saying

"Best leave now,
we're under control."

"But what happened?" I say to Milo,
as he pulls forward to swing around left.

I suddenly see two officers
guiding Dakota by the elbows,
ducking him
into a cruiser.

My jaw drops a fraction.

"It's the desert, Vera," chuckles Milo,
steering us out.
"Can't make a noise without
everyone hearing.
We'll all know the whole story
by morning."

Well, *that* was a shitty night's sleep.
I roll out of bed
and splash the crust out of my eyes.

I want coffee.

I don't drink coffee,
but I want that
carotid-artery-superflush this morning.

I get a clean tee
and climb into it,
slamming the drawer shut.

Someone knocks on the front door.

What the hell?
The clock says 6:47 a.m.
Another emergency?
I run to open the door
and there is Lon,
the intense rays in back of him

shadowing his face.

"Can I come in?" he says softly.

"No," I state,
glaring at him.
"I'm coming out."

I gesture for him to sit on the steps
and I see he has a flat brown packet
in his hands.

I stand in front of him,
and he raises an arm
to see me through the glare.

I move to the side.
I'm nice that way.
"Well?"

Lon's eyebrows are an anxious triangle.
He's trying to be vulnerable.

Vulnerable, my ass.
"I'm sorry, Vera," he says.

My arms are folded firmly
against my chest.
"Doesn't cut it, Lon," I snap.

"I know," he says,
looking down at the rocks
lining the path.
His brown hand gestures lamely.
"I was so convinced it couldn't be
any of the guys.
Dakota shot at me!
And missed, the idiot.
He's been stealing art and shipping it out
for a month. . . .
I didn't think it was him.
And here *you* were,
lost out here in the desert
and you were fazzed out

about your sister's death,
so smart and college-bound,
needed money maybe,
so it had to be you stealing from me,
and I was actually worried for you,
and then Milo stuck his nose in—"

"Don't you dare!" I interject.
"Don't you dare bring Milo into this!
You ruined his business
because you are still in fucking junior high
emotionally.
And worried, my ass!" I spit.
"A worried friend would have
talked to me,
not stolen my money,
not stolen my private postcards
and made fun of me.
You made *fun* of me
about my sister!
Is that how you treat people,

your family,
your guys?
No *wonder* they cheated you,
you immature prick!"

I glare at him,
leaning forward
having dumped the heaviest words
directly onto his black-feathered Native head.

Lon sits in silence,
and I notice the knuckles of his hand
gone whiter around the packet
as he listened to
my tirade.

"I'm sorry I thought it was you
stealing from me," he finally says.

I roll my eyes.

He rubs his hand flat against
the top of his thigh
as he sits,
palm on jeans making that
wooffft wooffft sound.
"I can't believe it

about Dakota."
Lon shakes his head slowly.

Then he turns to face me.
"But you have to admit,
you *are* fazzed out
about your sister."
He waves the packet at me.
"I'm sorry about that too,
that she died,
but you have to face
that you need
some taking care of."

I fix my eyes on his,
willing breath to come in a
slower rhythm.
"Are those my postcards?"
I ask,
teeth clenched
but not yet bared.

I snatch them as he holds the packet out.

Then I step lightly up the stairs
past him
and bring my packet inside
the Hovel,
locking the door behind me.

I feel cleansed
and weirdly elated
as I sit on the bed to undo the tape,
counting to be sure all
postcards are present.

I don't know how long Lon sat out there.

I don't care.

I spend the day cleaning
the Hovel,
sloshing white vinegar
over the kitchen counter,
vigorously scrubbing,
and happily splashing rinse water
everywhere.

The Hovel has never been so clean,
and probably
neither have I.

I am wiping out the drawers,
and as I heft my masher,
it hits me.
This masher
is the only thing
truly mine.
The fork is borrowed,
the dishes,
the pots,
the bedsheets,

the chair,
the outhouse,
damnit,
the whole house,
everything is someone else's.
Someone else's home.
Not mine.

I lean on the borrowed counter,
vinegared rag in my left hand,
my very own potato masher in my right.

Where is my solid rock?

Fake lemonade is almost strong enough
to cut through the smell
of white vinegar on me,
and I sit deep
under the back eaves,
watching the sun
melt down into the horizon.

Peg would have mixed
this crap lemonade with root beer
and called it
Lizard's Brew.
And Wendy and I would have drank it
and laughed our asses off
after finding out the stew she served
was made with seitan,
not real meat.

That Peg could cook anything.

And together we knew how to laugh

like there were
a jillion tomorrows.

I get my phone from the bedroom
and find Wendy's number.

Cross-legged on the bed,
I look through them one more time.

The girl in the embroidered dress
accepting the Olympic flame.

The flamboyant Strauss Monument in
Vienna.

The inebriated Dionysus.

The brigantine lifted by ice.

Funny how I continued
the Moth's tradition
of collecting postcards
but not sending them.

I don't expect her back.
I don't think I ever did

expect the Moth to come back
to a place where her pressed pantsuits
    and charming manners
    and tales of sparkling parties
aren't compatible
with the local scene.

Or with
two daughters in the sciences
and one lost at sea.

Taking the book of matches from the counter,
I bring the four postcards outside
into the dark.
In a flare of heat
they curl on the dirt,
the picture of the ship still glowing
after the others settle to ash.

The Hovel looks desolate
in the radiance of morning,
and I am glad I don't have my camera
because I'd want to take a photo
and that would
ruin
everything.

In my pack is a small jar
of gravel and dust from Main.

Milo will send my stuff at some point,
the drawer of postcards
and my new brilliant red mashed potato bowl
signed by the artist.

His truck is idling on the road,
and I get in the passenger side,
looking back at the outhouse,
starting to leak tears again.

"Aw shit, Milo," I say, laughing.
"When do the tears stop?"

Milo smiles, shifting gears to go uphill.
"Oh, they don't.
They do eventually stop hurting so much as they
come out."

I gaze at the relaxed line of his cheek
and think of his partner Jacob,

and I have to believe him.

Getting on the bus is easy.

Milo is standing in the bed of his truck
in the convection-oven wind of Baker
so he can see in the bus window,
flourishing both hands
like a joyous black widow spider.

He's yelling through his grin,
"Come back some time for pottery lessons!
Mud is geology, too, you know!"

The bus's air brakes release.
I sit with a thump into my vinyl seat
and we're groaning toward the distant highway.
Milo struggles onto the truck cab roof,
vigorously waving
smiling me onward

blowing a kiss as the bus turns.

And that is hard.

At the stop sign
on the far side of town
someone is standing,
waiting to cross.

The long dark hair
catches my pulse,
holding it still.

She turns to wave
up at the window,
and as I see her face
I notice the small boy in the seat in front of me
grinning and waving back,
and it jolts me
that this girl
is not
Amy.

And that
it will
never
be
Amy
again.

I wave to the girl
as we pull
away.
She doesn't
see
me.

As we do the diesel roll out of Baker,
I glance at my phone.

Three bars of coverage.

I punch in the numbers
quickly
before I think again.

One ring.
Two rings.
Thr—
A hoarse whisper comes through,
"Hello? Hello—oh don't hang up—Vera?"

I stare at the steel supports of the passing
billboard.

GUNS-R-US

One tear slides over the chapped skin
of my cheek.

“’Roley?” I whisper back.

I'm pretty tired of crying
    even keeping-it-quiet crying
in a bus
with total strangers,
but there's no one in the seat
next to me,
and I can't seem to stop the flow.

I rest my aching forehead
on the jouncing cold window,
letting it rattle my thoughts
into some order.

I feel sad.
I feel sad for 'Roley,
especially because I realize now
she was truly worried
all this time.
She has taken care of me
in her own kind of way
for years.

Because she had to.
Because the Moth was not there.

It just wasn't the sort of
taking-care-of
I want.

Not her fault.

That cherry cleanser smell
wafts up to me
from the bathroom at the rear.

I feel sad for Amy.
And guilty
because I never tried
to talk to *her*
about her drinking and crazy friends,
I just complained to 'Roley.

Sisters should talk to each other

about important shit.

And there I was
yelling at Lon
for not communicating with *me*.

Well,
Lon deserved it,
too.

Frickin' noncommunicating-handsome-
half-Hopi.

That makes me smile.

And a vision of Milo
waving good-bye from the truck,
that makes me smile.
And then cry.

My eyelids ache.

When I get to the darkening campground
with my pack,
nervous
and buzzy-brained,
I feel my cells regroup
to shore up my tired self.

I hear a whoop from the fireside
and Peg is sprinting over,
grinning like a joyous demon,
wrapping her arms around me,
"You're here! You're here!"
and Wendy is right behind her,
knitting in hand,
hugging me one-armed
with a yodeling "Wahoo!"

I tell them I don't have any camp gear
and Peg yells
"We can share!"
and Wendy says to come and have some dinner,
joking

"It's tofurkey casserole on the menu tonight!"
and we all laugh,
and the director of research comes up
and whacks my shoulder,
"Glad to have you back! My expert in
measurement!
We're finding great things here at the caldera!"

The rest of the team
raises ginger beer bottles
in greeting.
I wolf down my chicken curry,
Peg catching me up
with tall tales,
Wendy knitting and rolling her eyes.

It all feels so good,
so familiar.

When Peg gets up to use the latrine,
she says,

leaning down in her cowboy hat,
"We want to hear everything
that's gone on with you.
Sounds rough
and we're here to share it."

I tear up,
feeling goodness.

Wiping my eyes on my sleeve
I smell the dust and grit
behind me.

A moisture-laden breeze
tosses branches overhead
and I breathe deeply.

Wendy puts down her yarn
and rubs my upper arm once,
smoothing goose bumps,
looking into my eyes.

"Welcome back, Veer," she says softly.
"It is so good to have you here,
my friend."

And I feel I made the right decision.

I have re-
placed
my
self.

"Long Valley Caldera, California—View from the Northeast Rim"

DEAR ROLEY,

HOME CAMP IS MARKED ON THE PHOTO. WORK IS FUN. FOOD IS FANTASTIC. SUCH A WONDERFUL PLACE—AN ENORMOUS BOWL OF RUMBLING MOVING SOLID ROCK. SEE YOU SOON.

LOVE, VERA

Acknowledgments

Thank yous to

Catherine Frank, my editor,
who saw bedrock in this story through all the scree on top
while I was sliding around in bare feet.
Thank you for bringing my hiking boots,
the shovel,
and a bucket of ice cream.

Nicole Strasburg, my great friend in travel and art,
who adventured with me to Death Valley,
and didn't think it was odd when she found out
I hear voices.

Lynn Becker, Laura Covault, Dan Hanna, Siri Weber Feeney,
R. L. LaFevers, Mary Hershey, Valerie Hobbs, and *Lee Wardlaw,*
all members of my two writerly groups,

who supported me through, oh, everything.
Wasn't there a *lot* of everything?
Whew.

George Chaltas, my brother,
who gives the most fabulously entertaining
crib notes on any opera you can think of.
And some you can't think of.

Wendy Robins, Peggy Hogan, and *Pearl Francis*,
staunch friends,
who are always always always there
in the various forms I need them in.
Wendy, your reference in this book is to a woman who
is grounded in all she does.
Peggy, your reference in this book is to a woman who
is authentic with no embarrassment.
Pearl, your reference in this book is not literal (!), but to a
woman who
knows herself, pushes through adversity, and perseveres.